Legends of Elements

by Philipp Conrad

Author: Philipp Conrad
Verlag: tredition GmbH, Hamburg
The rights for the following text belong to Philipp Conrad, 19.12.2016.

Chapters

Prologue   4

A question of discipline   6

The valley of Eriandor   19

A long awaited meeting   37

Raging winds   54

A lovely evening   69

A water wipe   89

Rest   104

Embers   123

Return to the little things   140

Biting Cold   161

The calm…   176

… before the storm   192

Epilogue   209

Prologue

People often talk of four elements: Earth, water, air and fire, but this is not the truth. Instead there are six elements: water, air, fire, ice, earth and stone. They are present all around our world. Whether you search in the realm of man or in the realm of the elves, even in the realm of the dwarves. An old legend, but also an often told story from elderly man, even tells about old temples, all hidden in sacred places of this world, but where these temples are? No one knows for sure. There are clues and notes about these temples, but hidden and not well known. There are also stories about how this world got created and even those stories involve the six elements. In my youth I've been often told about stories of the elements, but I was a foolish person as I believed in the four elements, not in the six elements and I never really cared about the elements. But now that I'm older and wiser I often think about the tales of the temples and even the… other things… that are told about them. Even though

I'm telling of my youth as a foolish little boy, I find it kind of sweet to see the children run around and play like they would be god of the elements. Sadly I can't remember everything from my youth, only now I can remember the old stories that I've been told. Maybe I won't know anything about my childhood after all this is done or I'll remember everything when I'm an old man. Then I'll be sitting near a warm fire place, hear the children play and think about my lovely childhood... hopefully.

Chapter 1

A question of discipline

The sun was sinking, sinking into the sea, people would think and they would be surprised to see it again when the sun rises again. A carriage with a dark figure leading it were on a narrow road leading through a dense forest. They have been on this road for a long time. The dark figure turned around, but there was nothing to see on the road either way, except the endless look of trees and bushes of this land.

„We should rest here.", said a man in a dark blue cloak, „We shouldn't meet any other merchants or travelers this night. For this night is cold, colder than other nights I know, but a fire should warm our bodies and hearts for this night. Let your horse rest and make yourself a comfortable seat. I'll find some lodges to make a fine fireplace."

The carriage stopped and an elder man stretched himself and yawned. He was standing tall and breathing deep. It was a long ride for him and yet they haven't reached the town they seek.

The man laid down and looked up the trees to their branches and to the red sky which would be filled with stars soon. Again he took a deep breath, then he sat himself up and looked into the forest to search for the man who accompanied him on his way to Landriel the greatest city in this world for merchants, for the city is known for its great market which would be filled with people daily. But also for their fruity wine (which tastes like you'd eat 6 different fruits at the same time) and their fresh fish, which comes from the best fishers of the Basilisk Islands and from the Freed Island. Every man and woman wants to have been there at least once in their life. For our lad it's the first time in this land.

Then his companion came back from the woods with long and dry logs in his hands. His coat is dirty but he is used to it, he told him. He knelt down on the cold earth and placed the logs on the ground. Then he used a firestone to lit the logs on fire. Soon the logs were in flames and suddenly the night wasn't so cold anymore.

„I always liked it near a fire. It does not only warm my body but also my heart. It kind of strips away all the bad thoughts I have and I can only think of the good things that have happened. For me, it takes all the bad things from this world.", said the elderly man. He isn't so old as he seems, for he doesn't have any grey hair, but he is older than his companion. But he does have a dark mustache, unlike his companion, who only had some stubbles on his face. The coat suited the old man well and it had the same color as his hair, a brighter black.

„This is a really nice thought and I'd love to know this feeling too, perhaps it comes with the age. Cause I don't know this feeling."

„If I remember correctly, when I was in your age I haven't been so often near a warm fire place. In our home it was always cold and thus I may now enjoy my time near a fire place."

They both looked into the flames, as the flames flickered the merchant stood up and walked to the carriage. In the mean time the other man placed his sword in front of his knees and then he closed his eyes. The elder man returned and looked confused at the kneeling man before him.

„Excuse me Sir, but what are you doing there? I've never seen a person like this.", the old man asked him.

With closed eyes the man spoke softly: „Probably cause I'm the only person who does this or who has learned this. I'm concentrating, training my senses. I'm looking out for dangers that could harm us this night."

„Then why aren't you looking with your eyes and instead listening with your ears? How could you be so sure, that no danger would come in this night?"

„Everybody knows how to see with their eyes. They've done it for so long, they couldn't even imagine what it would be like to not see with their eyes. Some people in this world know very well how it is to see with your other senses, as they never knew how it is to see with their eyes.

„Who taught you this? Who was your teacher?"

„I was my own teacher. I learned this when I was eight years old and I was just about to become nine. In my hometown the elder men taught us kids how to hunt in the forest with bow and arrow. I was terrible with the bow and arrow. I could see my target, but while I would pull the string and let it go my target was already long gone. The other kids would laugh at me and my father wasn't proud of me. On some festive days our town would have a tournament for us kids. I never took part in these, on the wishes of my father. That's when I tried something different: I closed my eyes and started to breath deeply, then I started to concentrate on my ears and other senses. I tried to hear the sounds that my target does and from where they come. It took me very long until I could find my target, but I was able to find it and then I would hit it before it noticed me. On another festive day I took part in the competition and used my new way of finding my target. Surprisingly I won the competition. My father then came to me and said: ‚Son, you've made your father proud.‘. This was one of my happiest memories of my childhood. I'm not only doing this to train my senses, but also to remember myself of the easier times, when I'm currently in a hard time. But do not worry, for I did this now only to ensure our security for the night!“

„Then I hope I didn't disturb you?“

„No you haven't. I couldn't her any ominous noises and if there would be any danger, it wouldn't be able to find us until the next morning and until then we would be long gone."

„Happy news have reached my ear. Then I shall rest now. Good night!"

„Good night!", the elderly man fell asleep, but not his companion, who goes by the name of Darian. His parents are currently still living in the realm of man, in Darians hometown. He meets them every once in a while, when he has the time. He would love to meet his parents again, but right now he doesn't have any time to spare, as he has a long road ahead of him.

He watched into the flames for a long time. The cracking of the logs filled the forest. Sometimes he looked after the sparkles flying into the air and then fading away. But soon he laid down too and closed his eyes, but this time to relax his senses, not to train them.

The sun rose anew. The reign of the stars ended for this time and the sky colored itself red. They are back on the road again and walking to Landriel. The animals of the forest woke up and the birds started to sing their hymn. It is said by the elves that where ever you are the birds have a hymn. In some regions they're different, but all the birds of one forest know their hymn. When Darian first heard this story, he tried to remember, if the birds in the forest next to his hometown had a certain hymn. Surely they did, but Darian couldn't remember it for certain. *‚The next time I come home, to visit my parents. I should look after the birds and their hymn.‘*, were his thoughts.

„Is it true what they say about the cities and towns of the elves?“, asked the merchant. He was sitting on the bench of his carriage with the reins in his hands.

„I must apologize, for I don't know what people are saying about the elven cities.“, said Darian.

„You don't? I thought especially you are a person who knows all the stories, which are told in the streets. Nonetheless they tell that when the sun shines, the elven cities look like a forest and you wouldn't even know that you are in an elven town, if you were standing inside one. But when the night comes over the forests, when the fires are light in the chimneys, you would see thousands of lights in the trees once you look up. I heard these stories in Goldkeep and I wondered if they're true. You have to know this story warms my heart and gives me the will to travel to the elven cities."

„I hear many stories but I can't remember all of them. Thus I couldn't recall this story. But this story is right. When no elve is on the street you can't tell wether you are in a forest or in a city of the elves and at night the thousand lights shine through the branches. It must be an astonishing view for a bird to fly over a city during the night time. When I first saw an elven city during the night, I couldn't speak anymore and I immediately had the wish to be in one of these houses and sit there with them."

It has to be said that the realm of the elves is mostly a forest, that's why the story tells you can't distinguish between a forest and an elven city. The elves live in huge trees, but the king of the elves apparently doesn't live within a tree, instead he has his own palace. But there was once a tree, for the elven king, but King Ralind was so kind, that he decided to offer the tree to elves, who just recently lost their homes. These trees have an ongoing staircase inside of them. The elves have an easy way of life. In the morning they're coming together to eat, then everybody does what he desires. Mostly the mother and her kids are going to the market or meet some friends, then the kids can play with the other kids. The father is usually going to the forest to collect some logs or he goes after his duty, to earn the needed money for his family. You're probably asking yourself now, why do they collect logs? Well the elves do have a chimney in their trees, but these chimneys have a special separation from the rest of the tree, so the trees can't catch fire. Apparently there are poor and rich elves, but they don't call each other poor or wealthy. The only elven family which distinguishes it from other elves, is the family of the king, as they have many servants and are also guarded by many elves. The seat of the elven king is in Vasindrul, being situated north-west from Landriel.

„Then I hope that we will arrive at night! For the feeling of a warm place is the loveliest of all." and suddenly the old man, whose name is Girabel, felt strong and full of power, for he wanted to see an elven city now more than ever before.

„Well I can't tell you if we'll arrive at night. But you should experience this magic, as I guess you'll stay for some days, am I right?"

„Of course! You don't have such a chance twice in your life and I'll gladly take it!"

And thus they walked on for the rest of the day. They've met some other merchants on the street and exchanged stories about times full of happiness and joy. However there was an incidence, where one of the wheels of the carriage broke, but thankfully they came across a craftsman, who was able to help them and repair the carriage.

When the sun has sunken again the two travelers were just about to enter Landriel. They were greeted nicely by the elves and the story became reality in Girabels eyes. It lifted up his heart and although he has visited the elven cities for countless times Darians heart was lifted too. Probably due to the happiness in Girabels eyes. The lights remembered Darian of the sparkles of a fire, but these sparkles wouldn't move and only fade away, once the sun rises. They went on a path and on both sides were huge trees as high as the clouds, with white trunks and green leaves. The elves started to go back to their homes. There were no guards in the city, which was a strange look for Girabel as all the cities of man have guards on the paths, but the elves trust each other so they don't need guards on their streets. Sometimes there actually are guards on the road, but this only during special occasions. They were silent until they've reached Girabels accommodation, then Darian spoke with a soft and saddened voice: „And thus our paths will separate from each other. I have to go on, for I seek an other place than this city, but I'm glad that our paths found each other. Farewell!"

„This is a sad announcement, but go as you wish, knowing you made the life of an elder man merrier. Farewell!"

Now Darian went on the path through Landriel lonely. Some time he found himself standing and looking with his eyes into the tree branches to see the thousands of lights. Between the branches you could sometimes see the stars, if it's a cloudless night and your walking on the main path of the city. Many elven cities have a main path, from which you could see the stars for the branches of the trees don't reach completely over the path.

Landriel wasn't a small or a big city, it had many roads and paths to discover, but the people know each other as they often meet at feasts or on the market.

It has to be said that the elves have hundreds of special days which they celebrate and for each one of them the whole city meets and celebrates the day. One of the most heart warming days is the day of *Zivot*, the day of life. They celebrate life in all it's variations, they would sing a certain song and some say they even worship a god, which was long forgotten in the other realms. The day of *Zivot* starts with a special breakfast, with mostly fruits. Then all of the elves would leave their homes and go out. There they talk with their friends and take a stroll out in the woods, but they don't take the main road. Instead they go deep into the woods, to see all facets of nature. For lunch they mainly eat warm bread and drink fruity wine. Then the elves go to the main celebration near the biggest tree of the city. Dancing, singing and meditating are mostly practiced there, during this day. The celebration goes until the day has ended and the next one begins. The day of *Zivot* was introduced, during the Autumn Sickness of 355. Many elves were in a deep depression and everywhere were ill thoughts within the minds, the reason for the sickness is unknown, but soon help was coming from an elve called Zivolta. He created this day to remember the elves, about the good things in life, the actual beauty of life and it worked.

Soon Darian stood before a stable in which 4 horses were resting, two complete black ones, one white horse and a brown horse, with dark hair on its neck. He paid for one of them. He took the brown one with black hair on his neck. He wanted to know if the horse already has a name, but he decided to rather give him a name, once they traveled for some time. Darian mounted the horse and he galloped the long street down out of Landriel and he made his way up north.

Chapter 2

The valley of Eriandor

It was the second day after he left Landriel, when he entered the realm of the dwarves. The realm of the dwarves is smaller and there aren't as many cities compared to the realm of the elves and man, cause the realm of the dwarves is recognizable by its many mountains. There's only one place in the realm, which hasn't any mountains and this is the Plane Island in the east of the realm. The dwarves rather use their lands for agriculture, then for big cities. So there are many pastures in the realm of the dwarves. Though the realm is filled with mountains, it surprised Darian every time, what an astonishing landscape the dwarven realm has to offer. His journey was very quiet, as he didn't meet many dwarves on the street. But he met one dwarf: seeking some shadow underneath a seldom tree. Next to the dwarf was a small carriage, loaded with small stones. The dwarf was sweating, understandable for his work is hard and the sun burns on ones skin on such days. Darian asked him, if he was in need of some water. The dwarf gladly approved and Darian gave him his water. The dwarf took a sip and thanked Darian, but he didn't stand up, instead he kept lying on the ground and Darian laughed once he heard snoring coming from the dwarf.

One day later Darian was about to reach the river of Emlir, but he had to rest for sometime, as both Darian and his horse were tired of all the riding, so Darian searched for a good resting area. *If we won't find a place, where we wouldn't get washed by the rain, then we could swim through the river.,* Darian thought, but they were lucky as they found a small and dry cave near the path. „This is probably a common used cave by travelers. Here is some rest of a fire, probably from half a day ago, but this is strange, it seems to me that this was a bigger fire, a fire which should rather warm four or more persons and here is a trade of some horses, they had to stand outside in the rain.". But Darian wasn't concerned about this, for his eyes were just about to shut and his muscles were nearly asleep. Also he didn't sense any danger connected with the fire and if it were any outlaws, they're probably already gone beyond the next mountain. So Darian fed his horse with a carrot and then he laid down, closed his eyes and passed into the world of dreams.

The next day started and Darian was full of power again. Darian looked at his horse and it seemed, as if they both woke up at the same time. Soon they were on the road again, still on their way north. It wasn't long before Darian heard water flowing through hills and mountains. He had to ride over a stone bridge to cross the great river of Emlir. It is truly the greatest river on this continent, it flows through the realm of man, dwarves and elves. Its name comes from Emlir Terast, who first sailed along the whole river and founded the greatest city at the river called Ril-de-sur. Darian visited the city only once and that only for a short time, yet the city fascinated him and he hopes to visit it again someday. There are many legends about Emlir, for example that he used magic to sail along the river, that he was the master of the winds or that his ship could never sink, but

Darian doesn't believe any of them, he only thinks that Emlir was a marvelous sailor and he was in favor of the gods.

The bridge he crossed was wide, so wide that six horses could walk next to each other, but it wasn't the biggest bridge leading over the river, instead it was an abandoned bridge as it wasn't guarded by dwarves and even the moss was growing out of the gaps between the stones. Normally the bridges leading over the great river would be guarded by dwarves, at least the ones that are important for merchants or travelers. Darian used this bridge mainly to cross the river unknown and to travel faster. If he would've crossed a guarded bridge, he would've waited very long before he would even come to the guards and once he would've reached them, he had to explain who he is and what he wants in the dwarven realm. Everywhere Darian looked he could only see mountains, the river behind him was a nice variety for Darian and for his horse. In front of him were two paths, one of them goes up to the mountains, the other one to the bottom of the mountains. He didn't took the mountain path, for he knew that his destination was at the bottom of the mountains.

The path was long and rocky and every here and there he saw a *Quaril* or how man would call it: „oversized goat". These animals are so big that they could match a pony, yet dwarves are able to ride them and their horns are as sharp as a spear. The dwarves use them as war beasts and for transport, while man ride on their horses and use them to pull their carriages, the dwarves use the *Quarils*. But these animals aren't dangerous, unless you hurt them or they feel in danger, then they would start swinging their horns at you. The elves call them untamable, for they are too wild to ride them and Darian agrees them, for many times he saw a dwarf trying to ride them, but the dwarf failed and got thrown of the *Quaril*. Darian respects them as much as his horse or other animals and he respects the dwarves, who are able to ride them.

While Darian rode on, he thought of his last time he was in the realm of the dwarves. It was four years ago, he was in the main city Krenn-so-ul. Where he was to meet his friend Mari. Mari had bright shoulders and a stone grey beard that went until his hips. He is one of the strongest dwarves, Darian had ever the pleasure of meeting. They are good friends and together they went on a lot journeys through the mountains of Zilura. There they told stories about themselves, before they got to know each other. Also they experienced the wildest adventures in the mountains, Darian even found out that Mari is a former spy of the king of the dwarves, but he was dismissed due to his old age. They thought he was too old to serve the king, that he wouldn't have any more power in him, but this isn't true, as Darian has experienced.

The mountains rammed through the clouds and it almost looked like a dense fog up in the mountain path and Darian could feel that the air was moist. He went on, until the path went briefly down. Darian now looked down to a valley, where no stone could be found, no trees to cut down or bushes to harvest. Darian sighed: „Well here we are my fellow, the valley of Eriandor. This is a foul region, for there lies grief on this land.". He felt that his horse wanted to respond with silence and it did, while they were in the valley his horse wouldn't make any sound.

Around 200 years ago a battle took place in this valley. A battle which would wipe out an entire folk from the face of this earth. The battle was the last stand of a folk called *Duende*. The *Duende* were small creatures with a crooked back, their skin was rough and they had black dots on their backs. Also they were a very peaceful folk, but when they had to protect themselves they used pointed blades, which also where crooked. But they knew nothing of bow and arrow, which would seal their doom. They were experts in agriculture and had the best vegetables in the whole world. They lived in the regions near the river of Emlir and in the mountains around it. They lived until 687 in complete peace, but then the dwarves declared war on them. The dwarves accused them of settling within the realm of dwarves and represent a threat to their way of living. The dwarves burned their villages and salted their fields. The *Duende* fled into the valley (now known) of Eriandor. The dwarves came from the north on foot. The *Duende* were only about 300 and still they were able to kill nearly half the army of the dwarves. It is known that the *Duende* were one of the best fighters in the world, although their frail anatomy, they had a formation, which was nearly unbreakable, but after the ultimate defeat of the *Duende* the dwarves copied this tactic and use it nowadays. But in the end they were all killed, due to the arrows of the dwarves, which were a complete surprise to the *Duende*, as they never knew what bow and arrow could do. To honor them, the dwarves called the place after the last *Duende* that lived, before they killed him too.

Darian rode on with silence, thinking about the fallen on this field. In the mud he noticed more footprints from horses. „They are fresh. Probably from some hours ago.". Then Darian felt a shock all over his body, the footprints went to a small canyon to the right, they might lead to the same destination that Darian has.

He went on with a grim look on his face, for he expected this adventure would be a lonely one, especially in regions like these. Near the end of the canyon were two huge, flashy stones with a gap between them, big enough for Darian to walk through. When he looked between the stones he could see a dim light far away, deep inside the mountain. When he looked up he was clear, that this was his destination, for there were foreign symbols on a stone above the stone doors. Darian could only guess, what these symbols mean, he thought of: „*Here lies one of the great temples of elements. Every benevolent men or women is welcome here. "*

Darian dismounted his horse and said to his horse with an easy voice: „You wouldn't like it in this temple. You'll need to wait here, but don't be afraid! I'll come back. Be easy, rest for the time I'm gone, for when I'll return there will probably be another long ride ahead of us."

As he walked into the cave, everything got dark before him. There was no light in front of him anymore. He lighted up a torch and held it in his right hand. He walked slowly and silently down a dark and wet path. As he went on he felt the cold creeping on him, but there was nothing he could do against it. He only had his torch, which contributed only some warmth.

The path went on and on and Darian never saw the lights, which he saw before. Unlike before the walls are now flat and plane and they were marked with different symbols, Darian couldn't read, Darian assumed them to be a poem. The legends which tell about the temples, also tell that on the walls are many symbols, which form a poem or a story from a time long ago. The path took a turn to the left and to the right, as he looked into the left path. There he could see, that there was a person with a torch in his hand and a sword at his side. The person searched for something in the room, but Darian didn't want to know for what the person was searching for, he only knew that disturbing him wouldn't end well for himself. So he decided to take the path to the right.

He silently went on until Darian stood in a great hall. It was so big that you couldn't even see the ceiling. *This hall must probably fill in the complete mountain*, he thought. The torches of the hall were burning, cause of the host that arrived before Darian. They must be the persons, which rested in the same cave as Darian did. They stood all around the walls and looked at them. *Definitely more than four.*, Darian thought. There were even other silhouettes, but he couldn't recognize them. The walls had symbols on them again, but Darian couldn't read any of them. Darian stayed in the shadows and cleared his torch, he didn't want to get noticed, not yet.

There came a voice from a guy, who unlike all the others didn't search the walls, instead he looked on a thin paper in his hands, it had strange formed lines on it. „Did you find anything?", he shouted.

„No sir, only wet stone and some moos here and there.", said a small man with short blond hair.

„I hope you all remember what I said! We'll only leave this place once we found something valuable or something that provides us with information about the other temples.", his voice was very angry and soon rage would fill his complete body, for there came ill news, but not only to him, but also for Darian.

Two men in brown clothes and swords on their hips came into the great hall. Darian was lucky to squat behind a small stone wall, which served as a balcony within the hall. The stone wall saved him from the looks of the two men that came through the same entrance, as Darian did. One of the men looked exhausted, as if he was running for some time and he had to wipe away the sweat from his forehead, even his dark hair was wet. The other man, who was the person Darian saw before in the path to the left, started to talk with a nervous voice. „We've got company. Our boy Eric here noticed a horse in front of the entrance, but he couldn't find a rider and so did I, although I guarded the hallway.".

„Then find him, you idiots! We don't want someone, who ruins our work here.", said the man with the map. Darian could see that he has a dark brown full beard and he has long hair, which is bound together, at the back of his head. Once the two men walked away, the man with the map shouted more commands at the rest of the host.

Darian was now nervous too, as they knew he was there. He hoped that the host would leave soon, so that Darian could look around the temple without getting disturbed. He looked around the hall and could see that the balcony continued around the hall and that only the shadows laid there. Around the balcony were also pillars towering up to the ceiling. He walked around it and tried to look on the walls. There were these symbols again, even the pillars of the balcony had them, but Darian didn't find anything too. He looked down to the host again. They still searched the walls and the leader became more and more stressed and nervous, until he spoke again with anger. „You three there, you stay here and search in this hall! All the others come with me, we'll walk down this path. Maybe we can find something there. And you three come to us, as soon as you find something helpful!". The leader went down the path, with his host and the other silhouettes. The sounds of horseshoes echoed in the hall. The three men looked anxious at each other, cause they knew they aren't able to find anything here and their return to the leader wouldn't be so pleasant.

Darian saw stairs leading down from the balcony to the end of the hall to the path, through which the leader vanished. He slowly went down the stairs and followed the host down the path, unnoticed by the three men in the hall. The path split again, one way to the right, the other to the left. From both ways Darian could see a dim light. Darian didn't knew which path he should take, but in the end he decided to go the left path. He could hear the echo of the steps and voices of the host. Suddenly the steps fell silent and Darian halted. He awaited that any moment someone would spot him in the shadows, but it didn't happen.

Instead something very unexpected happened, at first there was a big growl and then screams came from the hall behind

Darian. Some men from the host ran down the path to the hall to look after their companions. Darian knew they would find him, if he kept standing there, he drew his sword from his back and ran back to the hall, he didn't want to spill blood on this floor. Suddenly there was a quake, from which Darian fell to the ground. There were sounds of horses coming from one direction, but Darian wasn't able to hear from which direction. The men didn't ran to the hall anymore, instead they ran into the other direction. Darian used his sword to stand up, he felt something flowing through him, as he put his sword into the ground. Knowing that his opponents are escaping Darian continued to walk down the path.

There were more screams this time from the other path. Darian had to hurry for the danger seemed to come closer, but he had to find some information, where to find the next temple. He came to a round stone wall with symbols on the wall again. They are different then the other symbols. These were more like drawings. There were tide lines which probably represent air and a moon with circles around it. Darian was thinking for some time, then he knew what they should represent. „The Basilisk

Islands!", Darian said. There were many more symbols, but there was another quake and Darian knew he had to go or he would get lost under the rocks, which would soon fall down from the ceiling.

Darian ran through the hallway, he saw a light at the end, but he halted when he was still within the shadows, cause outside Darian heard the host. He could see how they prepared their horses, some of them already sat on their horses. They must've taken them with them through the temple. Darian could here some voices.

„What is with the other guys? Are we not waiting for them?"

„No we won't.", Darian recognized the voice of the leader, „They are probably dead. Now go settle your horses! We have to ride for a long time!"

Darian waited for some time, until the host was gone. Once Darian was sure, that they left this mountain he stepped outside of the temple and stood in the valley path. He could see the mountain chain and how the sun faded away behind the mountains. He started to walk down into the valley, to get to his horse back. He wandered for quit a long time until he saw his horse again.

„Well, my fellow I'm back and I'm fine. You were probably worried about this guard that was here right?"

„Ay you! You there! Is that your horse?", it was the man, who spotted his horse and came running into the hall and reported the leader about Darians presence.

„Yes it is mine.", Darian answered.

„Alright then you come with me, I'll bring you to my leader.", he drew his sword, but Darian didn't.

„Well this will take you a long time, for your leader isn't here anymore. He left with his companions, a while ago. Put your sword away and I'll take you with me. I'll take you to an elven city, from which you can go your own way:"

„They're gone? Without me?… What does he want to reach with all these orders and in the end leaving his men behind… . But this is a great idea. You are a good fellow!". He put his sword back into its scabbard. Then both of them sat on Darians horse and they rode back to the realm of elves.

After one and half a day of fast riding Darian left his companion in Landriel, where the companion bought a horse and rode back to his family in the realm of man. Darian decided to rest in Landriel for a day. On the same day, that he arrived in Landriel, he went on the market to look for some provisions for his continuing journey. Fish, apples, carrots and some water, not only for him but also for his horse. He went on and looked at the stands of the market, there was mostly elvish clothing and food. But then there came a surprise to him, as he saw an old friend of him. There stood an elder man, with a bright dark coat and bright dark hair and mustache. As he turned around and saw Darian, a smile unfolded on his face.

„Well how nice it is to meet you here again! Just in the right time, as I'm about to leave within this day. What were you doing, while we didn't see each other?", Darian walked to him and greeted him.

„Well Girabel, I was in the mountains to search for something. What were you doing?"

„Oh merchant stuff. Selling food and leather, but also buying food from the elves and one of their famous wines for my family. I also wandered around to look at the beautiful life of the elves and their cities and it was one of the merriest experiences, I could have ever imagined. My heart is now ready for the journey back and it gets even better: I have an elve, who would love to accompany and share stories with me! Oh Darian, you can't imagine what a happy man I've become! Only through this small visit."

„These are marvelous news! I hope you'll have a happy time with him."

„I'm sure I will, but excuse me now, for I'm in a hurry right now" and so they wished each other farewell again and on the next morning Darian left the city again, but this time to the south.

Chapter 3

A long awaited meeting

The swords clashed and the sound of wood hitting wood resounded. The fight was long and exhausting for Darian. He was sweating, but his opponent was too. The swords clashed again and the opponents turned. Darian lifted his sword up to swing it down at his opponent. Then he swung his sword to the right, to the left and to the right again. There came a blow from above and Darian countered it. They turned again, trying to hit each other while they turned, but the swords only clashed again. He stroke from the right and his enemy tried to withstand his strike, but Darian brought up all his strength, which was left in him. His opponent didn't had any defense for a moment and Darian used this moment to strike his sword into his hip. It would've been a fatal strike, his opponent would've most likely died. They were panting, wiping the sweat from their forehead. Then his opponent started to talk, with an exhausted voice.

„I see you've improved your skills and trained a lot. Know that you're even better than I am."

„But still you are one of the best fighters I have ever encountered. It was a hard fight for me, as you can probably see, I am sweating all over my body.", Darian laughed.

„Yes, I can see that, but there is another robe in my lodge. You don't need to wear your leathern clothes, while you're with me.", Darian didn't wear his dark blue clothes, but instead sand-yellow robes, which were comfortable and easy to wear. There weren't any belts on it. They were an easy clothing and thus he walked to the lodge and clothed himself with the fresh robe. Darian and his companion were on a big hill. On one side was a long and beautiful landscape, there weren't any trees on the landscape as they're near the coast to the Never-resting Sea. On the other side was the ever ongoing forest of the elven realm. There led a way from the bottom of the hill, far up to the top of the hill, until you would come to a small temple, which was build by the elves as a place of peace. They weren't at the top of the hill but on a flat level of the hill below the temple. This flat level has enough place for a garden, a place to train and a small wooden lodge.

His companion was a long friend and teacher of Darian, he was an elve with dark blond hair and he had a bright smile. Though he is an old elve, his skin wasn't wrinkled, which actually isn't common for the elves, not even for old elves. He has the same robes as Darian and he lived in the wooden lodge. He moved away from the towns and cities into the hills and mountains, to find the peace inside of him. He has a young face, but he isn't very young, instead he is old enough to have seen two wars, which tremendously impaired him. That is one of the reasons why he moved into the hills now, to live in harmony with nature, the true peace. He moved here twenty years ago and still he hasn't experienced all the things, which these landscapes hide. He went into his lodge to serve him and Darian some fruity-hot water in wooden cups. The elve and Darian really like this drink, it makes their hearts easier and it warmths their throats. Darian looked far away to the horizon, where he could see hundreds of hills, there were some bushes with some of the fruits, that are used for the drink. He could also see some animals, grassing over the hills.

„You know, even after all these years, after all our meetings. I always find this outlook more astonishing, than the last time I have looked at it.", said Darian to the elve.

„I know, it's a miracle how many beautiful things exist out there, which've been found and yet have to be. Would you like to accompany me for a little stroll to the top of the hill, Darian?"

„My dear friend, you know I can not deny an offer like that!"

„And this is one of the aspects, which I like about you Darian.", they both smiled, it was a relieving moment for both of them, as they haven't seen each other for some years, „It has been a long time, since I've seen you. The last time you were here you've been so exhausted, that you've slept for days. When you came to me again, this morning you looked exhausted again. Do you have something, that haunts you?"

„No not at all Wilur, but I have my reasons. You know I'm now in a time of my life, in which I'm involved in a lot of adventures and dangers. I am grateful for any time like right now. A time where I can enjoy life in all its ways or to just have an inner peace like now.", Darian looked at Wilur. Wilur kept his eyes on the path, his face had a worrying look, which was unusual for Wilur, „But I have the feeling that something poisons your heart. You worry about something?"

„You're right my friend. My heart is poisoned with ill things and my thoughts too, for my folk is at war again. Our king and the king of the dwarves seem to declare a war due to the smallest reasons, which isn't right to their minds. Now it's about a small watchtower at the great river of Emlir, on the border of our realm and the realm of the dwarves. They can't decide wether there should stand a watchtower of the elves or of the dwarves. You know I've seen war and what comes with it."

„I know, but there has been ill blood between elves and dwarves for many years and of that you know too."

„Yes and there has been spilled too much blood on this beautiful world. Taking someone, who is a stranger to you, this wonderful gift of life is the biggest crime in this world. No one has the right to take someones life, no one has the right to choose, who should live and who shouldn't."

„Why is there no king, that shares this thought? It's a shame that there are so few people, who share the same thoughts like you do. I would always follow your way of life, but as I have told I am involved in many adventures and thus I can not live your way of life entirely, but I have my one rule and I will stay to it until my last breath fades away."

„And I'm very proud of you for this, as you know. This is why you are always welcome in my home. Many wars have already passed and sadly many will follow. How many wars do they have to fight, until they realize how unnecessary these wars are? I hope I live long enough to witness such an event."

They've now come to the top of the hill, to the temple. They looked at it with respect. They knelt before it and shut their eyes, trying to find their peace within them. Time passes and as the sun started to sink, they stood up again, now with new power and happy thoughts. The sun begins to fade away behind the hills and so Darian and Wilur started their way back to Wilur's lodge.

Darian met Wilur many years ago, when Darian was still a small boy and when he was still living in his home town. Wilur was wandering through the realm of man and he came coincidentally to Darians hometown. Darian was currently hunting lonely in the forest. He was kneeling on the earth and had his eyes shut, he listened for any animals. He trained his senses by concentrating. But Darian didn't hear animals wandering in the woods, instead he heard Wilur coming closer to him. Thankfully Darian noticed the steps and didn't recognize them as animal steps, for otherwise he might have fired an arrow at Wilur. He looked up to Wilur, who was looking with an appraising look at him. They talked for some time, until Darian had to go home again, but before they departed Wilur promised him to write a letter, so they could stay in contact and they did. After many years Darian was grown enough to leave his home and he travelled to Wilurs home. There Wilur trained Darian in the arts of life, but also in the art of fighting. They spent many years together until there was another war, which meant the separation of Darian and Wilur for many years. In the meantime Darian travelled around the world and learned about many different cultures. When Wilur returned he was a saddened elve, two wars had their impacts on him, but he and Darian were glad to see each other again.

„Tell me my friend, why did you come to me?", asked Wilur in a quiet but strong voice. It dragged Darian out of the past and into the present again.

„It has been a long time since I have last seen you. I just wanted to meet an old friend of mine again."

„Don't make a fool of me! I know there's another reason why you're here. Don't try to hide it from me.", on one hand is voice got harder, but on the other hand there was still a touch of jokiness.

„Well you know me too well. You know of the Basilisk Islands, right?"

„Yes I've been there many times. They're wonderful in their own mysterious way, but they're also very dangerous, for there are heavy winds and storms, even on the Basilisk Coast you can feel the winds raging."

„I'm searching for something there, it should be an old temple, which is hidden from the view of the common folk."

„A temple? The numerous times I've been there, I've never seen a temple or anything, which could be a temple."

„Is there any place you have not been on the Basilisk Islands?"

„Well yes, I've never been on the Basilisk Coast, as some say that they hold even greater dangers than the islands themselves."

„Then the temple must lay somewhere on the Basilisk Coast. Thank you my old friend!"

„For you I'd do anything. But what is the purpose of this temple, that you seek?"

„I am afraid I cannot tell you about it, not yet. I will just tell you, that it is truly important for me to get there as soon as I can, for I am not the only person, who seeks after this temple. I will probably have to leave you the next morning. I will get some rest and then I will have to ride on, to the Basilisk Coast."

„And so it shall be! Now let us hurry, so that you can have a long rest, before your ride!"

„Nay! I will not need such a long rest and I want to spent some more time with you, before I leave again. Who knows when I will come back?"

They walked down the hill, but on another path than before. It was the path through the forest on the other side of the hill. The hymn of the birds could be heard and it truly was a different hymn then the one Darian heard on his way to Landriel. Wilur knows this hymn too well. He could hum and whistle it, if he wanted too, but he never would. Why? Cause when he would do it, it wouldn't be an iconic hymn for the birds of this forest anymore. Wilur knows this and that is why he doesn't whistles or hums this hymn. In the forest were some stone ruins with moos on them. Wilur told Darian that these ruins are from the first elves, the Ancestors. Wilur knows this from the notes of his grand-grandfather, who endured a journey around the world and made notes about the first elves. His name was Relior, he was a wise elve and was interested in the creation of this world and in the ancient histories. He wrote hundreds of notes just about the first elves, sadly most of them are lost in the world and now probably destroyed. Wilurs grandfather considered to find these notes, but he died as a soldier in the destruction of Ascar. Ascar once was an island in the south and it actually was the island on which the king of the elves had his seat, but then an earthquake erupted, destroying the complete island. No elve ever talks about this incident, as only few elves survived this incident, the king during this time wasn't one of them. It was a dark day for the elves and the rest of the month it rained constantly. And why Wilurs father didn't search for them, no one knows. Probably due to his duties, he was a royal soldier. Guarding the king, is a honor to the elves as only six elves can form the royal guard. They are every time near their king and barely get any sleep and they can't leave the capital to meet their families. So Wilur wasn't able to see his father for a long time. Thus being another reason for Wilur to find the old notes of his grand-grandfather Relior.

When Darian looked far away into the woods he could see a lone wanderer. „Do you see this figure there Wilur?", asked Darian.

„Yes I can and it's very odd to see someone so far out here in the woods. Maybe this person got lost and needs some help.

We should ask him, if he needs our help.", thus they went to the lone wanderer. The lone wanderer was an elve. He had a brown coat, which was dirty. He was walking for a long time. He also had some fresh scarves in his face. He looked weary and anxious, as he noticed Darian and Wilur. „Hello there, my dear fellow! May I ask what an elve like you is doing so far away from any town or city?", greeted Wilur him with a friendly voice.

He looked frightened and he stuttered: „H-h-hello. I-I-I'm just a wanderer here in the woods. I'm on my way to the top of the hill. I've heard that a temple is located on top of it. Is that right?"

„Yes it is my fellow. But if you're just a wanderer, I'm wondering from where you got these scarves, for they seem fresh and there aren't any wild animals in these lands. You must know, that I know these lands.", said Wilur.

„I-I-I'm a deserter. Yes, a deserter from the war in the north.", he said confidential, but also frightened. The elve trusted Wilur. Both Darian and Wilur noticed it.

„My dear fellow, don't be frightened. There's no reason to feel like this. I know how you feel, I know what you've seen. I'm also a deserter in a certain kind of way. I understand you for fleeing from war and death."

„You are? Well then I'm alighted. Are you living here?", he looked astonished now and took of his hood. The elve had high cheek bones and a sharp chin, his hair was brown, brown as the wood.

„Yes I am, my name is Wilur and this is a good friend of mine, who goes by the name of Darian. I have a lodge just down this way. Do you want to join us? We have it warm there and you can drink, eat and rest there, if you'd like to!"

„Bless you, sir! You are a good person. You shall go on and I'll follow you!", then the elve had a smile on his face again.

They walked back to the lodge and drank some more warm-fruit water and enjoyed their time together, for soon they would depart and not see each other for a long time. While the elve ate and rested for some time. Darian and Wilur told stories about what happened, while they didn't see each other. Wilur was most of the time in the hills, but he also wandered through the elven cities. He now has seen every elven city that exists today. He also travelled to the Freed Island and met some of his old friends, there he also got the receipt for the warm-fruit water.

The elve suddenly woke up and yawned. Now Wilur wanted to talk to the elve and Darian listened to them. Wilur had a dark-green coat in his hands and he looked sad at it. „How is she?", asked Wilur and the elve looked at the coat in his hands.

„The last time I saw her, she was well, but I haven't seen her for some days."

„Is she safe from the war?"

„Yes she is, she lives now in a city far away from the borders to the realm of the dwarves. Who is she, if I may ask?"

„My sister. Many years ago I had to leave her, as war raged and I had to fulfill my duty. It was a dark day for our family. A messenger arrived and ordered me to make my preparations, for we would leave in a short manner of time. I used this hour to bid farewell to my sister and mother. I've never been able to see her since this day again. I know this is hard for your heart, but I've got to know about this. How is the war going? Is there hope for a soon end?"

„I shan't say for certain, as I've left the war some days ago. I can only tell of the time when I still fought in it. I hope that it would end soon, but the last time I looked at the battlefield, all my hopes were crushed. On the hills I could see how the dwarves began to put their war machines in place to attack us. Our general ordered us to cross the river and take over the city on the other side, but I knew, if I would've done it I'd be dead now."

„Ill news I reckon, but alas! You're safe now, you're in a better place! The only thing you shall find here is peace, rest and friendship!"

„For this I'm very grateful! I'd like to go up to that temple. Would you accompany me?"

„Yes of course! But not my friend here, he needs rest and will wake up soon tomorrow."

„No need for concern! He shall rest, if he needs. If we shouldn't see each other again, then to you sir: farewell! May your road be easy!"

„Farewell to you! Find your peace and forget the ill thoughts!"

Then Darian went to bed and he dreamed of wonderful things. He was standing on a coast spectating the sunset, then there came a woman to him. She spoke with a soft voice and she laid her head on his shoulder. Darian couldn't understand what the woman said. Now they stood together looking across the water and suddenly something changed across the water. Darian didn't see what it was at first, but slowly the whole ocean got darker. Darkness was crawling over the water and soon it would consume the coast on which Darian and the woman were standing. Darian wanted to let loose of the woman, but somehow he couldn't. The darkness reached the coast and Darian stopped every attempt of escaping from the darkness. He stood there and waited for the darkness together with the woman. The grass was loosing its color and no birds could be heard. It happened very fast and Darian didn't feel anything. He closed his eyes and only saw darkness. Then he woke up.

He stood up and he could see how the elve and Wilur were asleep. He didn't want to disturb them so he went outside, where the sun greeted him. The air was fresh and filled him with power. Darian went to his dark blue leather clothes. First his dark brown trousers, then his black boots and the black belt and at last his dark blue upper part. He turned around and saw that Wilur stood in the doorway.

„I see that you're ready to leave.", he said with a sad voice.

„Yes I am.", Darian went to his kit, with his sword. He fastened it around his back, then he went to his horse.

„Never forget your rule. Go easy and ride fast! Go with peace and come back as soon as you can! Now farewell my dearest friend!", said Wilur.

„I will never forget it, you have my word. I wish all the best for you. Farewell!" and so Darian rode down the hill. He could feel how Wilur was watching him. When he came to the end of the hill he turned left and rode west to the Basilisk Coast. While he was riding alongside the hill, he looked up where Wilur's lodge would stand and he smiled with a little tear in his eye.

Chapter 4

Raging winds

His horse started to run slower. His horse was tired and Darian knew it. Even Darian himself started to feel the weakness in his bones. But he also knew the Basilisk Coast wasn't far away anymore, as he could feel how the wind started to become more powerful. He was in a forest, but this one was different than the other forests in the realm, as here rain and storm rule over the forest. It's very unlikely to find any animals here, but fallen trees are very likely to find. Darian saw the first one not so long ago. Now everywhere he looked were fallen trees and their roots were visible to travelers. The clouds gathered above Darians head and he could slowly hear the noises of waves pressing against the stony walls of the coast. The last time Darian travelled to the Basilisk Coast was three years ago, he took a ship to the Basilisk Islands, but he arrived too soon so he decided to take a walk along the Basilisk Coast. But he wasn't the only person on the coast on that day. Instead there were three elves, which travelled to the coast to admire the nature and its strength. He walked to them and they reflected how they're about to visit every extraordinary place of nature in this world or at least this is what they hope for. Some of these places are the Basilisk Coast and Islands, the Desert of Hope, which is situated on the Freed Island, the Icelands north of the realm of dwarves and the mountain chain in the realm of man.

Darian came to the end of the highlands. The hillside went straight down before him and he could see how the waves pressed against the stoney wall. Now his search truly began, for Darian now had to find the entrance to the next temple. First he climbed down from the back of his horse. He took his sword, a torch and some other materials with him and then he left his horse alone again.

Darian walked to the edge and looked down along the coast to find the entrance. There was nothing which would resemble something like an entrance. He walked along the coast, with a watchful eye on the stoney wall under him. It was stormy as it has always been on the coast and it will always be stormy. It was hard to walk, as the stormy wind were very strong. Darians dark brown hair and dark blue clothes were fluttering in the wind. Sometimes the wind was so strong, that Darian couldn't breath normally anymore. He moved his head to the side to at least try to breath normally. There were many grey clouds above him, but it didn't rain. On and on he went and only rocks and waves were to be seen. Darian was dispirited, for he thought that the host, which he saw in the first temple, has already found the temple and plundered it and that they're on the way to the next temple. He took a sip from his water to refresh his body. Suddenly he saw something strange on the hillside. A small slit was in the hillside and a narrow path, which could easily be overseen, following to the slit. Darian ran to the path and nearly slipped on the mossy ground. He walked carefully down the path to the slit. The slit now became wider as he came closer. The slit was big enough for Darian to fit through and suddenly he stood in a dark and long path.

The air was fresh and the walls around him were dry. Darian lighted up the torch, which he took with him. Once he could see more, he saw symbols on the walls, but these were different than the ones in the last temple. These were more fluent symbols, the others in the first temple were edged. After some steps the path divided into two separate paths. One went onward, the other turned to the right. In both of them lingered darkness and Darian didn't knew which one to take. In one of the paths waited a trap behind the darkness, which could bring Darians journey to a sudden end. He decided to go the way onward, but he walked slowly and carefully.

The ceiling went higher, the paths got wider and the path divided yet again, but now into three paths. Darian decided to go onward again. The air got very fresh and Darian could hear the waves from the outside clashing against the hillside, but he also heard some strange noises. Darian couldn't figure out, what they were nor from where they came.

The symbols were on the walls again and Darian tried to read them. The strange sounds got louder and louder. Darian looked behind him and he could see a light, way back in the path, through which he came into the temple. Slowly he saw a silhouette holding the light. He put out his torch and laid it down onto the ground. Darian silently went on to hide behind a corner. He did indeed reach the temple, before the host did.

The light got brighter and Darian felt nervous. He took a look behind to see, if there was a way to avoid the people coming from the entrance, but he could only see darkness and some rocks lying next to the walls, which probably fell down from the ceiling years ago. He looked to the entrance again and now he could see the complete host standing in the temple. In front of them was the man with the long dark brown beard and hair. His hair was bound together behind his head again. Darian was in lead, but the host caught up. There were about twenty men.

„Now I want everybody to search through this entire temple. You look for something which gives a person a big amount of power or ancient riches from the constructors of these ancient temples. No one dares to talk to me, unless he has found anything. Did you hear me?“, the leader said. The anger was either still in his voice or yet again in it.

„Yes sir.", the complete host screamed. Two men of the host took the part to the right, but the majority of the host went the same way as Darian did.

They separated from each other and everyone took another path. The leader came straight to Darian as if he would know Darian was standing there and watching them. Fear and tension filled Darians heart, there was no place to hide from the host. There was no way to go, where the host wouldn't see him. Darian was set in a trap. He had to reveal himself to the host. Darian went some steps back. He didn't value to be silent anymore. The fallen rocks were now next to him and when he looked back, he saw how the path turned to the left, but from the path came another light. Darian was cornered.

„Aye you there!", the voice came from ahead, „What do you think you're doing here?", he spoke to Darian, „How do you think you shall find anything here in full darkness? Where is your torch?", he came directly to Darian. He saw the torch of Darian lying on the ground, „There it is! But why did you put it out?", he yelled through the entire temple. He came closer and closer, just as probably every man within the temple, „Wait… I don't recognize you!".

It felt like the time paused for a moment and they just stood in the faint light coming from the torches of the host. A sweat drop was on Darians forehead and he felt the complete tension in his heart. The leader looked at him with narrow eyes, „Who are you? And what are you doing here?", Darian saw a big scar on his left cheek. The leader had a long brown coat and Darian could see the hilt of a sword hanging at his hip.

Darian looked deeply into the eyes of the leader. He knew from the look of him, that before him stood a fiery person not declining a fight, „I could ask you the same question.", replied Darian.

„Apparently I've asked first, now be a nice person and answer my question.", his voice was sharp, but silent like a dagger. The leader looked deeply into Darians eyes too. He did not only look at Darian. He rather absorbed every little movement of Darian.

„My name is Darian and I'm an explorer on my own adventure. Now you sir."

„My name is Belric Reever and I'm on my way to discover the secrets of this ancient temple."

„Then I hope you won't ruin these temples or spill blood on their floors."

„No, certainly I won't. Unless any of these buggers lies to me and I tell you: I'm a man of my word."

„So you don't trust your own men?"

„Not all of them, but from one I already now he's lying and this one is just here in front of me."

„Why do you think so?"

„An explorer with a sword on his back is a very rare sight in this world, don't you think so?"

„This is a dangerous world we live in. A man like me needs to defend himself from such dangers. What about you? Why do you need twenty armed men with you?"

„There are legends about these temples. Something shall protect them from miserly people. Who knows? Maybe one of my men is a miserly person. We also need to defend ourselves, as you've said it, this is a dangerous world."

„Then why don't you travel alone like me?"

„Cause I don't want to get in such a situation like you do right now."

„What situation? Meeting some companions for the road ahead?", Darian heard how one man was coming at him, behind his back.

„You call twenty armed men a company? I would've loved to talk longer with you, but apparently I'm running out of patience. Certainly you represent a thread to my adventure, so I have no other choice.", Belric and Darian drew their swords nearly at the same time. The swords clashed and Darian made a kick to the person behind him and a kick forward against Belric to get Belric away from him. Darian turned around and swung his sword to the man, who tried to kill him from behind. Their swords met each other again and again. Belric rejoined the fight. Darian took some steps aside, now he swung his sword from left to right, from right to left. The sounds of clashing swords filled the temple. Soon the complete host would be standing around Darian.

Suddenly a quake occurred, from which Darian, Belric and the other man fell to the ground. Darian stood up fast, he felt as if his body was filled with new power and strength and then he ran along the path his right, but soon he was stopped. Stopped by a great gust, which came from the left and it wafted into the path in front of Darian. There was also a gust coming from the path behind him, but it wasn't as strong as the gust within the main path of the temple. Men were lying on the ground and some flew to the path in the front of Darian, all due to the gust. One man was just about to fly into the path, until Darian caught him and drew him into the path, where the gust wasn't so strong. *Someone of the host must've activated some kind of trap within this temple,* Darian thought.

A big rumble came from the path in front of Darian, directly followed by screams from men. Shock and fear filled Darians heart. The man next to Darian breathed heavy and slide down to the ground. Understandable, for he just slipped away from death. Darian turned around. He knew there is only one path left, that he could go to hopefully leave this temple. As he turned around he had to discover, that Belric is already gone and the other man with him too.

He decided to walk back the path on which Darian just encountered Belric. With all of his remaining power Darian walked against the gust. It was very hard, not to slip away. His muscles hurt and again it was hard to breath normal for Darian. But he was able to make it, once he came to the center of the temple the gust faded away. He ran, for there was no given time when the next gust was about to strike. The path divided again into two paths, Darian took the right one.

In front of him was one of Belrics men. He raised his sword above his head, Darian blocked the sword and punched him into his belly, he turned around and drew his legs away. The earth rumbled again and from the ceiling rocks loosened and were about to fall down on the man, Darian just fought with. He grasped him by his arm and drew him away to a safer place.

The path went on and then the path ended in a round wall. This was the wall, which would have shown the locations of the other temples. But the symbols are very hard to identify and in this pure chaos Darian wasn't concentrated enough to identify them. There was a thin long line with some curves. It could be a coast. Within the lines was a single symbol for a mountain.

There wasn't any time left for Darian, so he turned around and saw that right next to the path, from which he came from, was the exit of the temple. The sounds of waves from outside got very loud. He ran to the exit and got surprised by a wave. Now his whole body was wet and water dropped on his dark blue leathern coat.

Voices came from the outside, Darian could only hear two words. *Home* and *ship*. Then there were noises of horses and noises of men screaming, but they came from the temple. More thin steps led to the top of the cliff again, but they were completely wet and slippery. One time Darian nearly fell down the cliffs. It started to rain and the drops hailed into Darians face. Once he came to the top of the cliffside, Darian could see how the host left the Basilisk Coast, but still there were 5 horses left. His horse wasn't very far away. He ran to his horse and his horse got excited to see Darian again. Darian tried to calm him. His fur was wet too. Both of them wanted to leave this place as soon as possible, so Darian prepared everything as fast as he could and then he would leave the coast. With one last look back, he saw how some of Belrics men left the temple. They didn't bother themselves that Darian was standing there, as they were too shocked about what they've seen and experienced in this temple.

One day and one night he rode until he came to a town. It's a lovely place, which Darian has visited every time he came near to it. Some of his dearest friends live here and he visited them every time he visited this town. An off-river from the great river of Emlir flows through the town. Around the river you can usually see fishers and small kids bathing and playing in the water, although it is very dangerous for them, as the river is very fast. One of the kids once got caught by the stream. It happened when Darian was about twenty years old and Darian saw how one elve jumped into the river and saved the kid. This was an influence for Darian. From that day on he wanted to be a person like he saw that day, a simple person yet a hero to the common elves, dwarves and man alike. But this happened only once and nowadays the parents of the children, which are bathing in the river, would wait next to a nearby bridge and watch out for them.

He arrived between breakfast and lunch, so the streets were slowly filled with elves. They started their so called ‚morning stroll'. The elves have three strolls per day. At first the morning stroll, then they have their after-lunch stroll and in the afternoon when the sun starts to touch the ground their night stroll begins. Every stroll takes a good amount of time, but it depends on the weather. If it rains the elves won't go outside, instead they'll meet in their houses and sit there together, talking and telling stories. The children would play together, but some children would go outside and play in the rain and when they're finished they'd come home, dirty and tired of all the running. These are beautiful pictures, which are no rarity in this town. This is a reason for Darians constant visits. He visits the town every time, when he is nearby and after the incidents within the last temple, Darian thought it would be the best choice to visit this town again.

But Darian wasn't in the town to meet some friends or to watch the elves taking their strolls. He was in the town to buy some provisions. For he had to prepare for a long ride. A ride which would lead him far into the west. He would ride into the realm of man and he hasn't planned any stops or rests during his ride. He wanted to find the next temple before Belric and his men.

Chapter 5

A lovely night

It was a cold and rainy night. The taverns filled with men, enjoying their free time. In the tavern of ‚Blue-Pete', people were greeted nicely and they already filled their stomachs with their favorite drinks. There isn't any drink, which this tavern doesn't serve. In the tavern are three chimneys distributed, so that their customers have it warm and have at least a glimpse of the feeling of home. There are many tables and benches, which are full of men with their drinks and some food. Torches hung at the walls and beneath the windows. In a corner of the tavern sat a man lonely, with a dark blue hood over his head. The hood casted a shadow on his face. He looked very frightening, so no one dared to sit with him at the table. On his table was a candle and a jug filled with some ale. He looked across the room. He searched the whole tavern for a person. But the person he searched for would find him, before he found the person by himself.

It was an old person. He had long white hair and a short white beard with some grey tones in it. With his brown eyes he looked at the hooded man with indifference. He had a small scar along his forehead. Slowly he walked through the crowd and grabbed into a pocket of his black cloth to bring something out of it. His eyes kept on the lonely man in the corner.

„This is what you've asked for. Is it?", he gave the man in the corner a small old book. On it's top was a map of the islands west of the realm of man. The man took off his hood to unravel his brown hair, partly touching his neck, and his now grown, but still short beard.

„It'll serve nicely. I thank you very much!", he pulled out of his coat some gold to pay the old person. The old person bowed and vanished in the crowd again. Darian took a sip from his drink. He opened the book, to read a little bit in it. There were loos maps and Darian looked at them. They were very old, but at least he could read them.

He looked across the tavern again. People didn't mind him, they were busy with talking and drinking. He flicked through the book and sometimes looked up again. It seemed to him, as if someone watched him from a corner and he wanted to keep these maps from any unwanted glares. In a crowded corner everything was silent suddenly and a hiss was going through everyones ears. Darian closed the book and looked into the corner. Somehow nearly everyone in the tavern was silent, until they started to sing a song. They started to sing a shanty. The singers had dirty clothes, so they must be sailors.

Kind friends and companions,
come join me in rhyme.
Come lift up your voices,
in chorus with mine.
Come lift up your voices,
all grief to refrain.
For we may or might never,
all meet here again.

So here's a health to the company

and one to my lass.

Let us drink and be merry

all out of one glass.

Let us drink and be merry,

all grief to refrain.

For we may or might never

all meet here again.

Here's a health to the wee lass,

that I love so well.

For her style and her beauty,

there's none can excel.

There's a smile on her countenance,

as she sits upon my knee.

There's no man in this wide world,

as happy as me.

So here's a health to the company

and one to my lass.

Let us drink and be merry,

all out of one glass.

Let us drink and be merry,

all grief to refrain.

For we may or might never

all meet here again.

As they sang, more and more people would join them. They looked as happy as their voices sounded. They would sing on for a bit and with their song they turned the tavern into a happy and joyful place. With another look through the tavern Darian felt like he was watched by someone again, but he couldn't realize from where the eyes looked at him or to whom these eyes might belong. He stowed the book into his bag where it is safe from the curios looks. He emptied his jug and prepared to go. As soon as he stood up a big number of people sat down at the table of Darian. Everyone with a jug in their hands and some even with mutton on a wooden plate served together with warm bread. The bar was completely filled, but Darian managed to pay the barman.

When he left the tavern the cold greeted him and he put his hood back up again. His black leather boots sank in the mud of the street. To his left was a long street, which would lead to the town center and to his right was a short street to the port of the town. Darian was in the town called the Black Harbor. The town is situated in the far west of the realm of man and it is the largest harbor city within the realm. At this time of the day weren't as many sounds coming from the port, as when it's daytime. Most of the sailors and workers of the port are either at home or drinking and singing in a tavern, usually it would be the ,Blue-Pete'. But this does not mean, that the port is empty, instead there are always some people left in the port. In the dim torch light Darian couldn't see very far, but he could see how on the other side of the street were three black clothed and dark looking persons. He turned left to walk to his shelter for the night. He planned that he would leave the city within the next day. It was a broad street and on both sides were houses made out of stone and wood, with torches at their doors. There was also a tailoring and on the house was a big sign hung with needles and threads. But the tailoring had already closed for the day. There was only a single light coming from one of the windows above.

„Hold it!", said a hard voice from behind. Darian didn't bother and went on, „Are you deaf? I said hold it! Hold it or your gold will be ours!". Darian halted and turned around. Behind him were the three black clothed men from the other side of the street.

„What is it?", Darian said with a calm voice.

„What are you doing here? Hm? Sitting all alone in a foreclosed corner? Trading with some old man and threatening him?", it was a brazen man with sideburns and hard looking eyes.

„I didn't threaten anybody."

„You don't want any trouble with the guards do you? Course you did! We saw the face of old Greg as he left you! Pale as raw chicken.", spoke a thin man with brighter hair.

„I don't want any kind of trouble with anyone!"

„Look boys on his back!", the last person said. He had a hood over his head, but he looked more or less muscly.

„Oh that's a sword, probably it's just some rusty old sword, which isn't even able to slice paper!", said the man with the sideburns and the others laughed, „Probably threatened old Greg with it!"

„Well I want to see old Greg's face, once he knows he got threatened by an amateur.", said the man with the bright hair. The men laughed again.

„Now what is it that you want from me?", asked Darian with a hurry.

„The thing that old Greg gave you!", said the hooded person.

„I'm very sorry, but I can't give it to you! It's very important to me!"

„Well as it's important to you. I think we'll only rent it, for an unknown time.", said the thin man. They cornered Darian and came closer to him. They came into a small alley, where on both sides were wooden houses, through some windows shone a light and others were completely dark. He could see how one of them had his hand behind his back, as if he had a dagger in his hand. Darian casted aside the cloth to reveal his sword.

„Look his sword! That's no common steel! Seems like we'll take your sword too.", tension filled Darian and he started to grasp for his sword. He tried to look unimpressed as they came closer and closer.

„Move it boys! Or do you want me to call for the guards?", shouted a female voice, „Back of! He hasn't done anything wrong here! You can ask old Greg, if he really threatened him!", the voice came from a wooden house to the right, but there wasn't any light to see the woman.

„Who do you think you are? How do you want to explain the pale face of old Greg, as he left this one here?", shouted the hooded man into the darkness, while pointing at Darian.

„If you are so concerned about old Greg, then maybe you should give him some medicine. He is an old person and old persons become ill quicker, than you think!", Darian and the three other persons looked for the speaker to whom the voice matched, but there was no one to see.

„Do you know what you are saying there about old Greg?", said the man with the sideburns. Suddenly an arrow came flying out of a window. It flew right next to the face of the thin man and got stuck in a wooden pillar next to him. „Leave him or more arrows will fly and next time, they will hit their supposed target!"

With a sudden fear-consumed voice the thin man said: „Come Skrop! I think we should leave him! Also look at him, he surely can kill the three of us within a blink of an eye!"

Skrop, the man with the sideburns looked around the windows and then back at Darian. He stared at Darian. „Come on let's go.", said Skrop.

Darian laid the cloth back above his sword. A torch was lightened up next to him. The igniter of the torch was a beautiful lady with long black hair and a dark green dress. Darian immediately recognized her. „It's good to see you again Lira." he kissed her passionately, for it was the first kiss after nearly three weeks of not seeing each other, „Now where is your brother?", he turned around „Come out Isgur!". From the other side of the alley came out a young boy with short black hair and high cheek bones. He wasn't much smaller than Darian. He had a bow in his hand and with his other hand he put an arrow back into the quiver on his hip. He had a dark brown tunic and a small coat, tightened by a black belt. They hugged each other. Darians heart was filled with happiness and relief.

„I see you've trained with your bow.", said Darian.

„You think so? Although I've actually trained a lot more with my sword?", asked Isgur with enthusiasm.

„Well we'll see tomorrow, alright? Now how about we get inside?" and so they did. They entered a house to the right of Darian, as he looked around he saw three other doors. The entrance to the house of Lira and Isgur was a small brown door, behind two wooden pillars. Inside it was warm and homely. On the table in the middle of the room were several fruits and vegetables and three candles. Darian got out of his wet coat and his baggages. Isgur placed his bow and arrow right next to his sword in the cabinet next to the door. They seated all around the wooden table.

„Sweetheart I'll make you something to eat, you look very hungry.", said Lira.

„Thank you and yes I am indeed!"

„Now tell us Darian, where have you been and what brought you back here?", asked Isgur eagerly. So eager his chin nearly touched the flame of a candle as he leaned over the table full of excitement.

„Well I think I can give you a short summary. You probably heard of the legends about the elements?"

„The legend about the six elements, yes. Our parents told them many times, once we went to bed."

„The legends also tell of temples hidden in places no one knows of and well I've been searching for them, trying to discover their secrets. For the first temple I had to travel to the realm of the dwarves and ride through an ancient battlefield. I've already found two temples and I'm currently on my way to find the third one."

„What did you find there?"

„Lots of symbols on the walls and markings to other temples, that's why it's so ‚easy' to find them now. Apparently most of the markings to the other temples are not readable. Furthermore I've encountered in both temples a host of men.

Until now I haven't fully found out, what they're doing in the temples, but what I know is that the leader probably searches for golds and riches and he might intend to plunder the temples and thus I've got to get to the next temple before the host"

„And now what? Where do you have to go now?

„The markings led me here. I have to find an island in the Stormsea. But I don't know where it is. That is why I have purchased this book. Somewhere in here I should find the island I'm searching for."

„So this was the reason for the trouble outside?", asked Lira.

„Basically, yes. But old Greg did indeed look ill. Had a red nose, too. I hope he recovers soon.", Darian looked into the flames of the candles.

„He will, at least now he could afford some medicine with the gold, which you gave to him.", she smiled at him.

„Tell me how the island looks like and I'll look through the book and search for the island, for you. In the mean time you can talk a little bit with my sister. For surely, you two have a lot to talk about after three weeks."

„If you think so, then good luck with it. But come back to me, as soon as you find it! It should be located north west of the moon island and the island should have a very straight coastline, not many bumps. In the center of the island should be a single mountain, too.", Isgur instantly went upstairs and left his sister with Darian.

Lira just grilled a chicken for Darian and cute some vegetables. She seated next to Darian. They kissed again. „And what have you been doing here, while I was traveling in the world?"

„Nothing, besides cooking, scrubbing and worrying about your life."

„You worried about my life?"

„Indeed I have. But I'm glad that you're back."

„Me too… Me too."

„You won't imagine how many times Isgur talked about himself coming with you and outlive many adventures together with you.", she said with a laughter.

„Did he? Well I think it needs some more time, until he can come with me. He isn't ready yet. He still has to learn a lot about the sword fighting and I cannot afford to have him suffer due to a lack of skill." Darian sat there with Lira, who had her head on his shoulder. They enjoyed the brief time they had.

„Darian!", it came from upstairs, „I think I've found the island!"

Darian went upstairs. The stairs crunched, when he stepped on one of them. Upstairs he stood in a small floor with three doors. One door was open and in the room was Isgur sitting at a small table. „Here take a look!". The book was lying on the small wooden table. Next to the book was a big candle. There was indeed a small island, with a straight coast and on it a single mountain was marked. „This must be the island, Isgur! Well done!"

„However this book says, that on the island is only a mountain and a path into the mountain, which ends in a waterfall within the mountain. On the outer side of the mountain is another waterfall. There aren't any remarks on a temple."

„Well the temples are very well hidden. You can't just simply find them and thus there may be no remarking of a temple."

„What now Darian?", he asked.

„I'll have to find a ship, which would take me there."

„When would be the best time?"

„As soon as possible!", Isgur ran out of the room and down the stairs, „Where are you going?", Darian shouted downstairs.

„I'm finding a ship for you!", the voice of Isgur was followed by the sound of a closing door. Darian looked around the room of Isgur. There was a map of the known world and training dolls, which were already tattered. On the table were books. Books with stories about the history of this world and its places.

„ Do you see what I mean? He's very eager to go with you.", Lira was standing next to the door and looked around the room, „It's his biggest dream. Apparently he has to dream for some time on.".

„It isn't bad for him to dream on. Dreams are the things, which make us lively. Due to them we strive onward.", he sniffed, „Is this the chicken, I'm smelling?", he smiled. They both went downstairs again and Darian got his meal served. The chicken was very hot. Darian felt it in his mouth, as his tongue started to pain. Still it was tasting perfect, „It's really good."

„If you say so, then I'm relieved."

„How long do you think we still have, until I'll have to go?"

„Don't you mean until you'll have to go into the temple?", she had a bright smile on her face.

„You… You want to come with me? Did you really think about this? Out there everything could happen, like a storm or we could get attacked by the Black Sails."

„Well if we should get into some trouble, then I have still you by my side.", with all of their passion they kissed again, until they got interrupted by Isgur, who managed to find a ship, which would bring Darian to the next temple. They didn't have much time left, until they would start, cause experienced sailors know: When you start in the dark, the wind shall be with you.

„Sister where are you going?", Isgur asked as he saw Lira walking upstairs.

„I'll explain it to him, while you prepare everything.", said Darian and Lira nodded, „So Isgur, your sister will accompany me on my trip to the next temple."

„If this is so, then I shall come with you too!", he said it with a sparkle in his eyes, as he saw a chance for him to become a part of Darians adventure.

„You may come with me, but I'll have to tell you: It'll be very dangerous, even though you'll only accompany me on my trip to the temple, not into the temple."

„What? But why not into the temple?"

„Cause it's way too dangerous inside the temple and I'm yet not counting with the host, which might also be there. There are traps hidden in the temple, earthquakes also seem to occur inside the temples. If the host is inside the temple and we'd be there together, we are way easier to get spotted and get killed, as I can't look out for both of us at the same time. I feel sorry for you, but look at it with another perspective: At least you could join me, on my way to the temple and back from it and we might get into a small adventure, if you're aware of the dangers on our trip."

„I am aware."

„Then go prepare everything.", with that said Isgur ran upstairs and packed his belongings. Darian turned around, to his baggages and his sword. He sat down on the bench, staring into the fire of the chimney. The wood crackled and the sparks flew high and burned up. It reminded him of his time, with Girabel and he wondered, where he might be right now. Together with his family and kids and telling stories about his journey to an elven city? He might already be on his way to his next contract. Then he looked at his cup and started to drink from it. He heard steps from above coming downstairs and he knew: Lira and Isgur were ready to leave.

Darian bound his sword and baggages around his back. Lira blowed the candles out and Isgur tipped out a water bucket on the chimney, so that the fire died and now the complete room was filled with darkness. Both had one bag with clothes, except Isgur who also had his sword with him. They went outside and Lira locked the door. In the alley was it even darker then before. No light shone from the inside of the houses around the alley any longer. On the street were only two guards patrolling. Apart from them no other person could be seen on the street, except Darian, Lira and Isgur. It was very cold now and Lira laid a blanket around her shoulders.

As they walked past the ‚Blue-Pete‘, the tavern keeper closed his tavern. The smell of alcohol laid in the air.

They could already see the port and three ships, which docked there. Darian wondered, which one was the ship for their journey. Hopefully it isn't something too big.

„This one is our ship!“, whispered Isgur and pointed at a medium sized ship. It looked fine and the crew was ready to set sail. They went to the ship and the captain greeted them on his ship and soon they set sail for the next temple in a cold night.

Chapter 6

A water wipe

The wood of the deck was wet and the crew had some free time, as the wind and the sea were calm. On board were some boxes and strings distributed. The deck was relatively clear in comparison to other ships, as this ship wasn't supposed to transport goods or recourses. Isgur turned around and attacked Darian. He panted as he blocked the blow. Isgur attacked from the bottom and from the top, both of them were blocked by Darian. „Strike harder and faster!", Darian shouted at him.

They moved in circles, until Isgur attacked with a blow to Darians belly, Darian blocked the attack and after the block he tried to hit Isgur at his shoulder, but Isgur parried the attack from Darian. Darian expected the parry and moved away from him and stroke his blade to Isgurs back. „Now you would be dead.", Darian laughed, but Isgur didn't. He prepared for the next attack and hinted a blow from the left, but he attacked from the right. This surprised Darian a little bit, but he managed to stop the attack. He followed Isgurs attack by three blows from above, the right and from above again. Isgur sprang away from Darian and turned around to greet him with a heavy strike, which nearly disarmed Darian. Darian rammed his shoulder at Isgur, from which he grunted.

„A bit harder and my lunch would come out of my belly.", Isgur laughed and coughed.

„I know, but the enemies we'll face won't stop there, but rather slice through your belly. You did good, nearly had me two times.", Lira came upstairs from the cabins, „Have you finished your training?", she asked. Her hair was bound together to a plait. She also wore a dark brown dress.

„Yes, we have. What are you doing outside here? Breathing some fresh air?"

„That too. At first I wanted to know how long it lasts, until we'll arrive at the island. Secondly I just had the feeling to take a stroll on deck."

„Well let's ask the captain, how long it'll take us to the island.", they went into the captains cabin, which was situated between two wooden stairs. They knocked at the dark brown door. „Come inside.", shouted the captain. Inside was a dim light of a candle on the desk of the captain. On the desk was also a map of the world, with some other things on it, but Darian didn't know them. The captain has a wine red coat, with gold strands. He has red-brown long hair and a tousled beard. He spoke with a smoky voice. „What do you want, my customers?"

„We want to know how long it'll last until we've reached our destination?", asked Lira.

He thought about it for a time and looked at the map on his table, „We shouldn't be so far away from it any longer. We might get there this night. But I cannot say for sure, as I've never sailed to this island before. Wasn't even aware that it exists."

„Alright, thank you Captain Craver.", said Lira with a smile. They wanted to leave the cabin until the captain said: „Darian would you please stay here for a moment.", Darian turned around and looked at him. Darian turned to Lira and Isgur and smiled at them. „Then I shall stay for some time.". Lira and Isgur went outside.

„Please sit down.", he pointed at the chair in front of him. Darian seated down, it was a comfortable chair according to the circumstances. „What is troubling your mind?", Darian asked.

„What am i supposed to do, after we've arrived at the island?", he asked with a serious voice.

„Well I expect of you to wait at the island for my return, I guess."

„How long will it take you to come back?"

„I cannot say for sure. It can go very fast, if we are the only ones there. However if there are some other persons, it might take a bit longer."

„I can't wait there, for an unknown time. I'm a busy man and I have a lot of work in front of me. Also what do you mean with other persons? I hope you don't mean the Black Sails?". The Black Sails is a guild within the realm of man. They are known for terrorizing the sea and the towns along the coast of the realm of man. Once they sacked the town, where nowadays the Black Harbor is situated and thus the town got its name.

„No I don't mean the Black Sails. I mean other travelers. About your business I can only say one thing and I'm excusing myself for this rapidity, but your business right now is getting me to this island and back to the realm of man."

„I know, but such business has its price. The longer it takes, the higher is the prize. This was only meant to be a friendly reminder to you."

„Then I will remember."

„Then you are free to go.", Darian lifted himself up and went outside. It got darker outside. A big circle of crew members stood before him, he tried to see what is happening inside the circle, but it was hard to see past the heads and hands rising into the air. One hand nearly slapped Darians face. Soon he realized what it was. It was a fight and he was standing inside the crowd. Isgur was fighting some members of the crew, but they fought with their fists and not with swords. He left the crowd. It couldn't happen anything dramatic, for Isgur made new friends fast within the crew. They liked the innocence of Isgur and his will for adventures, an attitude always wanted on a ship. Darian looked for Lira, who was standing at the railing of the ship, enjoying the sea. The sun started to sink and thus both the sky and the sea started to turn orange. He walked to her and hugged here from behind.

„It's beautiful, isn't it?", she asked.

„Yes indeed."

„It makes you forget all the foul things in this world."

„It shows you the meaning of peace in this world.", they were both silent. But shortly Lira broke the silence.

„I love you, Darian."

„I love you too, Lira."

They stood there for some time, until Darian decided to go into his cabin, for he needed some rest before they arrive at the island. It seemed to him, as if Captain Craver was actually wrong about their arrival. Lira accompanied him, but Isgur was still playing and laughing with the crew and he would for a long time. Under deck no one could be seen, except for the cook of the ship, but he just enjoyed his free time and took a nap. So Darian and Lira went into their cabin, Darian blowed the candles out and closed the door. Together they laid down in the bed and closed their eyes.

Darian woke up and so did Lira. Isgur was sleeping very deep in his own cabin. There was a shout from above. „Land!". It was very dark outside and the stars shone bright in the sky. Darian went upstairs and looked at the island. It was a small island, with its big mountain in the middle. Unfortunately as Darian observed the coast line he saw the silhouettes of another ship, it was not bigger than the ship of Captain Craver, who stood on the deck with him. There were shouts from the crew: „Are these the Black Sails?".

„This isn't a ship of the black sails!", the captain shouted to his crew, „Now are these the travelers you mentioned?", asked Captain Craver Darian, who now tightened the belt holding his sword on his back.

„Probably", he answered, „You won't attack them, cause they probably won't attack you. But if they do, you may defend yourself. You understand Captain Craver?".

„If this is your wish, but come back fast.", he shouted at Darian as he walked back into his cabin. Apparently Isgur woke up from all the shouting on the deck and he was awaiting him at the hatch. „Are you sure I shouldn't come with you?", he asked. His face looked fine, he didn't carry any fighting wounds from yesterday.

„I'm completely sure Isgur. We now know the host is in the temple, which makes it way more dangerous, than it already is inside there."

„But also challenging, for one person alone."

„Isgur I know, how eager you are to come with me, but you need to have some more patience. While I'm inside the temple, you may train with the crew. I saw how well you did with me and with them. They like you. They could teach you something.", he left Isgur with a disappointed face. It was hard for Darian to always leave Isgur behind, but it's the only reasonable solution.

Lira was awake too. She was looking with a sad face at him. „Watch out and come back.", they kissed each other. Then he went upstairs, left the ship and landed on the shore of the island. Darian looked along the coast and didn't see any living thing. Rocks filled the island, but there was a path leading up to the mountain and around it. As Darian went along the path he noticed how the path, led to an opening in the mountain, the entrance to the temple or at least he hoped it would be the entrance. He ran up the path and looked back to the ship. With a deep breath he took the last steps to the mountain.

As he stood at the entrance he sensed wet air coming from the temple. He slowly walked inside. It was a small narrow path, the ground and the walls were wet. Unlike the other entrances to the temples, this one had unequal walls, with rocks piercing through. He heard water falling down. There must be a waterfall nearby and this waterfall was at the end of the path. *This must be the dead end, which stood in the book*, Darian thought. Truly it looked like a dead end. There was only a waterfall and nothing behind it, at least so it seemed. Until Darian stretched out his hand to the waterfall and to his amazement he didn't feel a wall behind the waterfall. He also didn't feel any ground behind the waterfall. ,The temple must go on behind the waterfall and it has to go some way down.', so Darian decided to swing into the temple with a rope. There was a rock standing out of the wall next to the waterfall and Darian attached a rope to the rock. He made sure it's firm and walked some steps back. Then he started to run at the waterfall. His heart was racing. He swung through the waterfall and due to the water splashing into his eyes he couldn't see anything besides darkness. Suddenly the sound of rope tearing apart sounded in Darians ears. At first he thought he just hallucinated it, but then he fell down into the water. The water wasn't as deep as one would think. If you would stand straight the water would nearly go to your knees. Under the water was a hard rocky ground.

It wasn't as high as Darian expected it to be, nonetheless his body hurt from his unplanned landing. Especially his side and his back hurt. He crawled out of the water onto a small stone island. He coughed. He was in a great hall, with many smaller and bigger stone islands surrounded by water, some of the stone islands had a pillar on them. There were two further waterfalls within the great hall on both sides of the them was another pillar. Darian tried to stand up, his whole body started to ache, forcing him to stay on his knees. There was a deep laughter.

„Well who do we have here?", Darian recognized the voice, „So primitive. Now all of you, go along the path and find something useful. Horas you have the pleasure of erasing this problem of ours.". Darian turned around to see how Belric and his host was starting to leave the temple. Only a big person in full armor was looking at Darian, on his back was a great sword. Darian was breathing heavily, as he fell down into the water again. He tried to stand straight, but it was hard to stand straight due to the pain in his back and side.

„I'm sorry. Shouldn't have cut your rope, cause if I hadn't this might have been a very good fight.", he laughed. He walked to Darian and pulled out his great sword. He screamed and attacked from above, Darian stepped away. Horas growled and started a series of attacks. Darian tried to dodge every single attack. He could feel how rage filled Horas heart with every missed attack of his. „Stop dancing around and fight!", he shouted at Darian. He attacked again and Darian again tried to dodge. Until Horas grabbed Darian by his belt and punched him in his face. He fainted a bit and his head now started to ache too. Darian managed to release himself, but he got a kick to his stomach from Horas, which threw him away, he landed again in the water. Now he was certain. He stood up, with pain in his face, stomach and back. Darian tried to hide is pain, with an angry look on his face. His coat was a big weight on his shoulders now. Horas only laughed at him. While walking to Horas, Darian pulled out his sword from his back. „At last he stopped dancing around.", said Horas.

They started to clash their swords at each other, every blow was hard for Darian and countering Horas attacks was even harder. Darian tried to push him away, so that he would fall on his back, but Horas was a single rock in the hall. During their fight they walked over several stone islands and through the entire hall, until they came to a pillar. Horas swung his sword at Darian, Darian however took some steps behind and Horas sword hit the pillar. Darian saw an opportunity for a good attack. Apparently Darians sword didn't got through Horas armor. His armor was as solid as Horas body as a whole was. They fought on and Darian got beaten up very badly by Horas. Darian even got hit by Horas sword at his left arm. The wound wasn't very big, but together with the pain in Darians body it was exhausting to fight on.

Darian breathed very deeply and hardly. His heart was racing and he felt as if he's about to pass out. His opponent wasn't exhausted or at least he didn't show it. Darian was about to attack Horas, as a quake occurred. Both fell down to their knees and suddenly they forgot about their fight, as they realized the power of nature. The wall behind a waterfall was crumbling down and from it came a great tide. Both Darian and Horas got caught by the tide and Darian passed out. At first he thought he was dead, but then he heard sound of water and rocks falling into water. Slowly he opened his eyes. Darian was now on the other end of the hall. He couldn't see where Horas was. He stood up and again he felt a mysterious energy filling his body as his sword touched the ground, but his whole body was still hurting. He looked at the wall, which crumbled down some time ago, but Darian didn't know for how long he passed out. He looked into darkness and wondered what would lie beyond it. There was another earthquake and from the darkness something moved into the hall. A big stone creature rose before his eyes. It was nearly as big as the hall and in its hands was a great spear. Darian didn't breath. It felt as if his complete body stopped working. This was the reason for the quakes and for the screams of the men in the other temples.

Darian now knew that the legends about upholders guarding the temples are true. Darian only thought how these legends purpose was to keep people away from these temples. He never thought how these could be true. He looked right into the stoney eyes of the giant, who wasn't standing far away from him. The giant turned his head at Darian and their eyes found each other, suddenly it looked like the eyes of the giant started to glow in a dark blue color. Silence was everywhere in the hall. Only Darians heartbeat and the the sound of water falling on the ground could be heard.

The giant started to run at Darian, with his spear ready to kill Darian. Darian on the other hand only knew he had to run away. He started to run into the only direction that he could go, to the last waterfall in the hall. When he was behind the waterfall, the giant ran slower, but Darian didn't. He only halted for a moment, when he reached the round wall. He hoped to find something, which would bring him to the next temple. The pain in his head effected his ability to concentrate. He saw a symbol resembling a mountain and on top of the mountain was smoke. The pain came again just like the tide in the temple did. The pain brought Darian almost to kneel down, but he remembered the threat of the upholder coming for him.

He ran on and before him came another waterfall. The sun blended him, it was morning again. He was beyond the waterfall and he couldn't see any ships at the coast. Suddenly Darian thought about all the possible scenarios: Did the host destroy the ship of Captain Craver? Or did Captain Craver leave him on this island, presuming him dead? Darian felt the cold creeping upon his body. He ran as fast as he could down to the coast and around the island to the other side. The pain was insufferable for Darian. Once he saw the ship of Captain Craver, the cold washed down of Darians body. For a moment he forgot all the pain in his body and he had a bright smile on his face. Then the pain returned and he collapsed. He only felt how he fell on the ground and suddenly everything got black. His last sight was the sky with its last touch of red. His last thoughts were dedicated to Lira.

Chapter 7

Rest

Lira, he thought. He stared into nothing but darkness. He returned to his dream of the coast, which was filled by darkness. He felt how he moved on the earth, but he couldn't see anything. The woman beside him vanished in the darkness. Everything was silent, nothing could be heard. No birds song, no waves looming over the coast, no sticks cracking underneath the paws of animals. Everywhere he looked was nothing, a huge emptiness filled the world and his heart. He didn't know where to go, but he knew he could only go on. He can't just sit down and wait for the darkness to vanish. Perhaps it would never vanish, then he would wait, until his life vanished in the darkness too. So he walked on, he was afraid, for he couldn't see what lays before him. With his hands he tried to feel anything around him, but there was nothing left. Until something strange was happening in the distance. There was something besides the darkness, something brighter. Then he opened his eyes.

He was looking at wood. Slowly he looked around and realized he was in a small wooden room and a candle was standing on a table right next to him. He was lying in a small bed. As he tried to stand up, pain grew in his body and forced him to lay down again. The door opened and Lira came into the room. „Darian!", she screamed, „You're awake!". She nearly fell down on him.

His mouth was dry. Around his stomach was a bandage and another one around his arm. „How long?", Darian stuttered. In his voice you could here the dryness of his throat. It sounded like croaking.

„For some time, but we're not far away from the island. We are on our way back to the Dark Harbor.", she took a wet cloth out of a bowl and placed it on Darian's forehead. In the bowl was hot water.

„I need to speak to Captain Craver. Now.", he tried to stand up again.

„Can't this wait for a moment? You've just woken up and you need some more rest!", now he was sitting on the bed, struggling to fully stand up. Lira seemed so reasonable, that Darian hesitated with his thought of speaking to the Captain, but it was important to speak to him.

„It cannot wait. It's urgent matters!", he was standing, but with some pain in his stomach. He put on a tight leather coat and went upstairs to the deck of the ship. The air was refreshing for Darian and the crew was looking at him, Isgur was looking too. Their stares were pinned at him He rushed across the deck, right into the cabin of Captain Craver. He was currently reading a book with a blue leather cover and on it stood *The story of Brack*. A common book under captains. This book is about a fantasy character, which is a captain too and he seeks for nothing but to return to his home, after his duty in a war. Darian heard sailors and captains often speak about this book, but Darian never read the book. Captain Craver roused up as Darian came in. He looked at Darian, with a whimsical look.

„Captain, I have to speak with you."

„Darian, it's soothing to see you standing upright again. Most of the crew thought, you wouldn't wake up until the we've arrived the Black Harbor again. Some even thought we may never see you standing again. But what is the manner of your rush?"

„You know the seas and their islands, Captain?"

„Yes I do, every good Captain should."

„Do you know an island on which a mountain is situated, which… smokes?"

„A smoking mountain?", he was thinking for a moment, looking down on his maps and books distributed over the cabin, „I don't know a mountain, which smokes. Unless you are speaking of a volcano? Cause then I only know one place and that is the Freed Island, on the very southern tip of the island lays a volcano. This is the only thing, which looks like a mountain and smokes."

„This must be it! How long would it take us to get there?"

„Take there? You don't mean, I should change our course to the Freed Island and sail you there?"

„I do and as you've said. I'm ready to pay you, even the higher prize."

„If you say so.", he stood up and went outside, together with Darian, „All of you listen. We'll change our course from the Dark Harbor to the southern tip of the Freed Island.", he turned around. „Thank you", Darian whispered to him. The captain only made a gesture with his hand and closed the door to his cabin. Quickly everyone was at his post and the ship turned to the right.

Darian looked at Isgur, he was standing there with a happy face or was it more of an uneasy face? His face looked like both and it made Darian fell uneasy, nonetheless he walked to Isgur. He saw in Isgur's blue eyes and Isgur saw in Darians brown eyes. They said nothing, there were only the noises you would typically hear on the sea and on a ship.

„Did you train with the crew?", Darian broke the silence between them.

„Indeed I have.", he answered, „What happened in there, Darian?"

„Would you come down into the cabin with me? So I can tell you and Lira the story.", Isgur nodded and they walked downstairs into their cabin. During their walk some members of the crew would look strange at Darian, as he passed by. In their cabin Lira was sitting on the bed, in which Darian woke up. Darian sat down on the bed and Lira took care of him. Isgur leaned to the wooden wall of the cabin.

„Isgur wants to know what happened in the temple and I thought I should tell you both of the recent events.", he explained to Lira, „In the temple I found the waterfall, which was mentioned in the book, you've read Isgur. But behind the waterfall wasn't a wall, instead the temple started behind the waterfall. The waterfall was only there to keep the temple a secret. I tried to get inside the temple with a rope, but the host expected me and cut the rope of mine, so I fell on the ground, but it wasn't so high. After this, the majority of the host left the temple."

„We saw them running out of the temple and getting on their ship.", Isgur interrupted him.

„One of them stayed in the temple. He was ordered to kill me, luckily he didn't, but he was near to. From our fight I got most of my injuries. However our fight got interrupted by a huge wave, which came out of the walls. Behind this wall was a giant, the upholder of the temple. He was about to kill me, but I was able to escape and strangely he didn't follow me any further once I've gotten out of the hall. As I got out, I realized no ship was standing at the coast and I had ill thoughts about you, so I ran around the island and as I got to see the ship of Captain Craver I passed out."

„When we saw the ship of the host leave, most of the crew thought you were dead and Captain Craver was just about to leave, until I could persuade him not to.", recalled Lira. On Darians face came a big smile.

„And we could feel a small earthquake, while you were in the temple.", said Isgur.

„This must've come from the collapsed wall and the great wave following it."

„What now Darian? What did you say to the captain?"

„We are now sailing to the south of the Freed Island, to the next temple. Which is probably hidden within the volcano, which is situated on the island and I just asked our friend to change the course."

„Are you sure about this Darian?", Lira looked worried, „You've barely survived the encounter within this temple and now you want to go right into the next one? And do not forget, this temple is in a volcano, from what I've heard about a volcano, it's already enough dangers without any giants in it."

„I am sure Lira, with your care I'm very sure.", he looked into her eyes and tried to comfort her.

With a sudden jolt, the silence of the room broke. They asked each other what this sound was, then another jolt came. Isgur ran onto the deck to find out what is happening. Lira walked out to the floor, she followed Isgur upstairs too. Slowly everything started to sway. Darian was alone in the cabin, but he tried to make the best of it, he tried to take a nap, but due to all the swaying this was nearly impossible for him. He stood up again, it worried him how Lira and Isgur weren't returning. He turned around to the door and saw a dark figure standing in the door. He had a small face, with some freckles around his cheek, and a long nose and he had blonde hair. From his back he drew a small knife.

„You don't want to do this.", said Darian to the man. He stared into the dark eyes of the man before him.

The man only said with a cold, but sad voice: „I must.", then he attacked Darian. He tried to stab Darian in the heart, but Darian evaded the stab. He grabbed the arm of his attacker and disarmed him. With a kick the attacker fell down on the ground. He crawled out of the cabin. Darian threw the dagger into the wood of the wall. The attacker found a sword on the floor and stood up again. Darians sword was next to the bed, apparently the bed was right next to the door, so he had to switch sides with his attacker to grab his sword. The attacker came forth and tried to plunge his word into Darian, but Darian jumped on the bed and grabbed his sword. With a single move his sword came out of its scabbard and swung at the attacker. The swords clashed two times before the fight would end.

Isgur came back from the deck and immediately wanted to attack Darians opponent, but Darian stopped him. The attacker kneeled down, as Isgurs sword was at his neck. He let go of the sword in his hand and Darian took it. Isgur looked at Darian with a confused look.

„We'll bring him to another cabin.", Darian looked at Isgur, „What happened outside there, Isgur?"

„A storm raging outside. I helped the crew."

„Do you know where Lira is?", Isgur shook with his head.

They went into the meeting cabin of the ship. The crew wasn't there, as they had much to do with the storm outside. Neither Isgur nor Darian knew where Lira was. „Isgur go search your sister, meanwhile I'll interrogate my attacker.". Isgur left the meeting cabin without any further words.

„Why didn't you kill me?", he asked Darian.

„Cause we need you and you don't deserve to die."

„But I was about to kill you."

„You were about to fulfill the order of Belric. I noticed you weren't eager enough to kill me, unlike Horas. You probably know him. On the other side I see you are a man with a family, a lovely wife, a child, maybe even two. You didn't want to go with Belric and his men, they promised you riches and gold, the reason you went with them. You only wanted to provide your family with gold, to live a good life. You didn't come to kill humans or get yourself in danger. Didn't you?", Darian looked deeply in his eyes. There was fear, but also relief, he might have found a safe way back to his home. He looked down onto the ground and his eyes searched through the cabin. He didn't answer, instead he thought very deeply what he should say next.

„There is no reason for your fear. I mean you no harm. I only want to know from you, if everything I just assumed is right.", the man looked up, into Darians face.

„I can remember exactly what he said: ‚You boy! I want you to get on that ship unnoticed. Take this knife and if it happens somehow, that this man survived. You make sure he won't live any longer. They'll might find you and kill you. But I won't forget your sacrifice, I promise. Your family would get all the supplies they need.‘, I've already guessed it, but now I'm certain he was lying to me.", hatred filled the eyes of the man.

„Calm down, they are safe, you are safe. You'll have to come with us for the moment, but I'll tell the captain, he shall bring you back home.", Darian looked at the man and then he thought for a moment, „If I might not survive my visit to the next temple. Take this.", he gave the man a small bag, full of coins from his baggages, „This is enough to feed a family for four weeks.", in his eyes was no hatred, but hope and joy.

„I... I... I don't know what to say. Thank you so much. I can't express how grateful I am."

„And you don't have to, my friend.", they smiled.

„But I won't travel with you back, as my family lives on the Freed Island."

„Is that so?"

„Yes, Belric recruited most of his men on the Freed Island. He thought recruiting men within the realm would be too dangerous. Before he recruited me I worked in some taverns just to gain at least some money for my family, but it wasn't even enough to feed me alone.", they remained silent for a moment, „I haven't told you my name. I'm Erich."

„My name is Darian. That is an uncommon name in the realm, but I wouldn't have known from where you come, if I have known your name before. Are you hungry? Here you can eat an apple, while I'll look after my friend.", Darian went upstairs to the deck. The storm was still raging, his clothes got wet very quickly. Shouts came out of all directions. It was hard for Darian to see anything, besides rain and his wet hair.

„Darian finally you join us out here!", shouted a voice from the right. Darian recognized the voice of Captain Craver. He looked to the right, he saw the steering wheel and then he saw Captain Craver standing at the wheel. He went up the wooden stairs to the wheel.

„Now what are you doing out here? You surely cannot help us right now with your injuries."

„I'm searching for Isgur and Lira, did you see them?"

„Isgur, yes! He was up here on deck and helped the crew with some of the ropes. Useful boy, I must admit. Then he went downstairs, since then I haven't seen him.", thunder rumbled and in front of the ship a lightning could be seen, Craver laughed. To strangers Craver would seem like a mad man, but in truth he just loves the sea and the storms. It's his home and the storm is just playing with him.

A person came from downstairs to the deck. The person was clothed in a dark coat, the person had blond hair. It was Erich.

„And who is that right there?", Captain Craver shouted, he looked at Darian with a strained look. „This isn't one of your companions. So who is this instead?". The man on the deck turned around to the steering wheel. „I don't know this man! What is he doing on my ship? Someone get this stranger off my ship!". A member of the crew heard him and was on his way to the unwanted passenger. Darian ran down the stairs. „Darian, are going to teach this man a lesson?", shouted the captain after him. The crew member drew his sword. Darian shouted: „No, do not kill him!". The crew member didn't stop. Darian rammed the crew member away. He fell down and Darian kicked his sword away. Darians new friend wasn't hurt, only confused just as seemingly everybody on the ship right now.

„Darian, what are you doing? You knew about this person being on my ship?", Cravers voice was angry. Darian answered with a single look to the Captain.

„Go downstairs. I'll do the talking.", with a nod Erich went downstairs again and Darian went upstairs to the captain again. Another thunder grumbled right after a lightning.

„What do you have to say in his defense?"

„He's one of my companions now.", with this Darian left and went downstairs. He felt the angry look of the captain on him, but he didn't care. Downstairs he found Erich sitting on top of a barrel. In the other side of the room was Isgur sitting on a bench with a hateful look at Erich. Darian walked to Isgur at first.

„Why is he still alive? He tried to kill you!", whispered Isgur, but his voice sounded as if he was just about to scream at Darian.

„You would be surprised, when I would tell you how many persons I killed.", said Darian with a strict voice, but his voice softened, „Did you find Lira?"

„She was on the deck, but as the storm got stronger she disappeared in the captains cabin to hide, as she didn't find the hatch to the cabins. She is now in your cabin."

„I'll go to her. The Captain praised your actions outside and I do too. Once this storm is over, you can show me the results of your training with the crew, alright?", Darian smiled at Isgur. He looked happy for a moment, until he saw Erich again. Darian walked into his cabin, as he got closer he heard sobbing coming from his cabin. Lira was sitting on the bed. She cried. Darians heart was instantly filled with grief and his knees felt like butter, as he saw Lira crying and as he heard her sobbing. He sat next to Lira on the bed, she laid her head on his shoulder.

„Why Darian, why?", she asked, „Why is all this happening?"

„I cannot say for sure."

„You didn't do anything wrong."

„I didn't yes, but I'm an impediment for them and men like Belric only have riches in their eyes. Men like Belric would do anything to get their riches. All this greed dazes their minds, it corrupts men, even kings.", he had to think about Wilur and his experiences in the wars, he fought in. „But not all people are like this and you know that."

„Yes I do, but it would be better, if there were more people with sense and less with grief.", he kissed her forehead. They sat there for a long time, with Darian comforting her.

The swaying stopped. Together they walked upstairs. The last grey clouds flew above their heads, the storm laid behind them. Relief could be found everywhere on deck, although the deck was a complete mess. Boxes lying everywhere and ropes hanging from the sails. The sun shone in everyones faces. The captain came down the stairs, as he left the helmsman with the steering wheel. On Cravers face was joy, he looked like a child coming home from an afternoon together with his friends. „Everyone of you deserves six bottles of rum and they all go on my account!", the crew cheered to his announcement, „Now to you Darian. Who was that person with the blonde hair?"

„ He deserted from the host and ran to your ship, but he knew once you would see him, you would throw him into the sea or kill him. So he decided to stay hidden, until I've found him. He will leave us, as soon as we'll arrive at the Freed Island.", he smiled at him.

Isgur came to the deck, with two training swords. He smiled at him. „You want to see my skills?". Darian grabbed one of the swords and now they were standing in front of each other. Craver went back into his cabin again. Darian immediately noticed how Isgur's skills have increased, he waited for him to attack. Darian attacked from the side to Isgurs hip. He blocked and instantly tried to hit Darians shoulder, following with an attack to Darians head. Darian moved away, turned around and suddenly Darian felt the cold steel at his arm. Darian looked up and saw Isgur standing with a bright smile.

„Now you would be dead."

„I would indeed. Who trained with you?"

„I trained with nearly every member of the crew.", he looked around the faces of the crew, they nodded happily.

„Boys you did a good job with him. You really got better and maybe…", Darian just looked at him trying to hint Isgur something. Isgur understood and on his face pure happiness unfolded. Darian gave his sword to one of the men around him and looked around the ship. The sea was quiet. *Remarkable how quiet it is, just after such a storm.* He looked at the horizon to the back of the ship. The grey clouds were still in the air, they mastered the storm.

Darian went downstairs again, where he found Erich talking to the crew. They're laughing. They're understanding each other, this made Darian truly happy. He went into his cabin. Lira was sleeping, the recent events costed her a lot of energy and especially for Darian, so he laid down too to find some rest.

Chapter 8

Embers

The air was heavy and warm and the volcano was looming up high in front of them. A mountain chain led to the volcano on his left side. Those mountains were small, compared to the volcano. It looked mighty and frightening at the same time. The earth was dry and with every step dust raised into the air. Darian turned around and looked at the ship of Captain Craver. They landed not very long ago, two days after the big storm. Once the lookouts noticed the volcano Darian, Isgur and Erich prepared to leave. Lira tried to convince Darian and Isgur to not go into the temple. „You are still to weak Darian!", she said to him. He didn't had all of his strength back yet, but there is no further time for him to wait. He has to go to the next temple, there was no other way. Darian and Lira kissed each other many times, before he left her, but Isgur didn't say goodbye to her. Isgur wasn't a man of farewells and goodbyes. Lira was anxious how both of them might not come back, but Darian assured her he will look out after Isgur and would make sure that Isgur will come back. Darian also spoke with Captain Craver before he left, cause he wanted to make sure they would wait for them.

They left together with Erich and together they walked for some time, but soon Erich had to leave them. He thanked Darian again, from all of his heart and he invited Darian to visit him in Treinta. „Once you come into the city, just search for a tavern on the right side of the sewer, which flows into the east, when you're standing in the market. There tell the tavern keeper my name and he will know what to do.". Darian smiled at him and he assured him, that he will visit him.

Darian turned back around and walked on, to the volcano with Isgur walking right behind him. He was wearing his dark blue clothes again. Darian is excited and anxious at the same time. It's his first time, that only Isgur accompanies him on an adventure. His breath became heavier with every step he took. Grey clouds were gathered above the volcano and they send shivers down Darians spine. He thought about what they might find in the temple. Belric and his men? They didn't saw the ship of Belric and his men. Maybe Belric is already on his way to the next temple? It was possible as the course of Captain Craver was at first in the false direction, which costed them precious time. Also they sailed into a storm, this might have slowed them down, but Darian didn't know. There was only one way to find it out. Darian could now hear Isgurs breath too and it got harder and harder. But he was still excited to be with Darian. For a moment Darian even had the feeling of passing out again. Ill thoughts filled his mind of failing on their adventure and they stumbled numerous times. „Darian! Look there on the left, in the mountain chain!", Isgur shouted at Darian. Darian turned to the left and his eyes scoured the mountain chain and then he saw something. Beneath the ground was something black in the mountain chain.

„It looks like a cave, if you ask me."

„Maybe it's the entrance to the temple?"

„I cannot be sure about that."

„Maybe it's worth a try? Nonetheless the longer we go on, the higher is the chance of us dying. We have to find some shelter soon and if this is truly a cave, then we have our shelter!", Isgur let Darian think for a moment, until he decided to search for their shelter. The nearer they came, the more they were sure it was a cave. They gained hope again, as they reached the cave. Fresh air came from the cave and once Darian and Isgur were in the cave, they coughed very hard. All the ill air got pushed out of their lungs and then they breathed deeply. The fresh air filled their body and they felt new energy within them.

Darian looked around the cave. It seemed as if the cave was going deep into the mountain. „Isgur, light up a torch. We'll follow this way into the mountain. Who knows where this way might lead. It might end up in our favor.", Isgur followed the order of Darian and gave him the torch, „Be prepared for what might linger in the darkness.", said Darian and then they walked through the cave. From the ceiling came water drops and these could be heard throughout the whole cave. The air got warm and thick, as if Darian and Isgur were outside again, but no exit could be seen. They slowly felt heat crawling up their bodies and the way through the cave got smooth, the walls were flat and the ceiling too. Darian went with his hand along the wall.

„Isgur, I think we've just found the next temple.", Darian wagered, „From now on, we'll have to be very discrete, as we cannot know what is inside the temple and now I know about one of the things, that is hidden inside these temples and you do not want to see this. You understand?", Isgur nodded. Darian snuffed the torch and then they walked on. Until there was a turn to the right and from the right came a bright light. They halted and looked out for voices coming from the direction. Nothing.

They walked on, with their bodies sweating from the heat and their hands on the hilts of their swords. Not far away from them the path took another turn, now to the left. The light got even brighter and they could hear seething. Darian looked at Isgur and he wanted to look like a man full of courage, instead Darian could see how Isgur was shacking and in his eyes was fear. „Is everything alright?", Darian whispered.

„Yes, I'm fine. Just curious what is behind the corner.", he simply replied. Darian felt uneasy.

Behind the corner, they could see the path becoming a bridge, over the light source of the temple. Also the path turned left in front of them, but they couldn't see much there. So they decided to walk to the stone bridge, but the bridge didn't had a railing. Darian swallowed and wiped the sweat from his forehead away. The light source blended him. Once he could see anything again, he saw right into a gapping pit filled with a red substance. Darian guessed it would be lava, Captain Craver warned him before he and Isgur left. ‚Beware Darian, inside the volcano is a rare substance called lava. It's so hot it melts steel within seconds.'. When he looked to the ceiling he saw dark grey clouds.

They were standing in the middle of the bridge, when from the end of the bridge, four men came out of the darkness. One of them was Belric. „Darian!", Isgur whispered. Darian turned around and on the other end of the bridge stood four more men. One of them was Horas. They must've hidden in the separate path, before the bridge. Isgur still tried to look courageous. Darian turned to Belric, standing at the end of the bridge, grinning.

„Darian. I expected you to come here, but I did not expect you to bring someone else with you.", Isgur didn't look at Belric.

„You expected me to come here? After your hound there, nearly killed me?", Darian pointed at Horas. Horas only growled.

„I did. I might've just recently got to know you, but one thing I already learned was that you are an eager man. Nothing could stop you."

„Thank you for your warming words.", Darian now grinned back.

„You said that you already got to know Horas, right?"

„Not very much. We exchanged only few words."

„Pity, but I guess the time has come for the both of you to become friends and then to leave each other. To go separate ways and the remaining one to leave in sadness and emptiness.", Belric said.

„This is a bad way of seeing this meeting."

„Yes it is, but then no one would be disappointed about the outcome."

„And now? You're going to kill us?"

„No, I won't. I have to travel to the next temple, as this temple doesn't have any valuable information or riches, as until now every the temple did. I actually start to think there aren't any riches or treasures in these temples."

„And this would make the recruitment of your men an useless investment and all this traveling would be a waste of useful time."

„And exactly thats the reason why I'm still traveling to the temples. Cause there has to be something worth the investment and the time. Who knows maybe this conversation was in the end just a waste of time. So goodbye Darian and goodbye to your friend.", with these words Belric went into the darkness again, his men were following him. Except for Horas and the three other men. They had drawn their swords. Darian turned around and said to Isgur: „Stay behind me Isgur!".

Darian started to walk at the four men and while walking he drew his sword from his back. Horas looked unimpressed. The three men attacked Darian and he parried all three of them. Two of them were now behind Darian, ready to kill him from behind, but there was still Isgur, who killed one of them and quickly attacked the other. Darian was unpleased. In front of him was Horas. Horas charged at Darian with a battlecry. Darian stepped aside and turned around. He saw how Isgur killed the second man and was now fighting with the last remaining one. Horas turned around too and attacked Darian. He countered and hit Horas on his side, but his armor was too hard. There was only the sound of steel hitting steel.

Darians heart raced, just as his thoughts raced through his head. He remembered the fight with Horas in the last temple. He thought how this fight might end up the same way, as the last one did. With this thought he was about to command Isgur to escape without him, but then another attack of Horas came from above and he had to duck. He also thought how Belric again has a head start.

There was a scream, from the last remaining man of Belric. Now there was only Darian, Isgur and Horas left. In Darians heart was a shimmer of hope, maybe they could survive this fight and get out of the temple soon. Darian and Isgur stood next to each other, in front of them was Horas. „Well at least, this fight is getting interesting.", he roared and attacked both of them. They turned and Isgur slammed his sword at Horas back, still there was only the sound of steel hitting steel. Horas turned around quickly and grabbed Isgur at his left arm. He wanted to hit Isgur with his helmet, but Isgur was too small for him and Darian rushed to them and tried to hit Horas at his head, so he had to let go of Isgur to block Darians attacks. Isgur came to Darians aid and together they slammed their swords at Horas, but still Horas gave no sign of exhaustion. Their fight went on and on. This fight was longer than the first fight of Darian and Horas and frequently the sound of steel hitting steel echoed in the hall.

Darian attacked Horas many times, until he grabbed Darian at his left arm, he pulled Darian to him and punched him in the belly. Darian tried to release himself, through attacks of his sword, but there was only the sound of steel hitting steel. He noticed in Horas armor small lines, where there was no armor. These places without any armor were under his arms, around his neck and at his hip. Horas let go of Darian turned him around and kicked him. Darian stumbled and nearly fell into the seething lava. Darian had to cough, due to the punch of Horas to his belly.

Isgur was now fighting with Horas. Isgur frequently attacked Horas and Horas frequently attacked after Isgurs attacks. Then Isgur saw a chance of hitting Horas at his side. Darian tried to stand up, with the help of his sword. New energy filled him and suddenly he heard the sound of steel piercing through flesh. Darian looked at Isgur and Horas. Darian let go of a shout full of pain, as he looked at the picture of Isgur standing there with a sword through his belly. Horas laughed and it sounded like the devil in Darians ears. Horas started to push Isgur to end of the stone bridge. Darian started to run at Horas. His eyes focused on the small line at Horas hip. The sound of steel carving through flesh resounded again. Horas groaned and Darian turned around. Blood was coming from the small line in his armor, still he tried to push Isgur off the bridge. Darian attacked Horas's sword hand with all of his strength. Horas groaned again and let go of his sword. He stumbled backwards. Darian caught Isgurs's falling body. Horas was laughing again, suddenly a quake occurred and from it Horas stumbled so far backwards, he fell of the bridge.

In his arms Isgur was coughing and looking at Darian. Sadness was on both their faces. „Isgur, what have I done? Why did I take you with me? This is all my fault.", Darian said, swaying Isgur in his arms and tears rolling down his cheeks.

„You fulfilled my dearest dream of coming with you and going on an adventure. Thank you.", his words branded into Darians mind. Slowly the light of Isgurs eyes faded away. Darian couldn't hinder himself to cry. His tears fell on Isgurs dark brown clothing and seeped in it. Light was no more in his eyes. Darians heart felt empty.

He slowly drew the sword of Horas out of Isgur. With a small, but a strong throw the sword landed in the lava too. Isgurs sword was lying next to him. Darian grabbed it and put it back into Isgur's scabbard, he did the same with his own sword. He slowly stood up and carried Isgur's body in his hands. He slowly started to walk to the end of the bridge. On the bridge were still the corpses of the three other men. Who would mourn over them? Their families, but until their families would receive the message of their deaths a long time would've already passed. He walked along the path through the temple, looking at Isgurs corpse in his hands and trying to hold back more tears, but the loss was too heavy.

Although his thoughts were about Isgur and his fault of his death, he also reminded himself about the next temple. He walked together with Isgur to the wall, where there would hopefully be the markings to the next temple. In his mind was the picture how it should've been: Isgur standing next to him. *It's my fault,* he thought. On the wall was a round marking, which looked like another island. ‚You fulfilled my dearest dream of coming with you.‘ In the round marking were symbols for mountains (or so guessed Darian). He might have to look into the book again, through which they found the island with the last temple. He remembered how excited Isgur was, when he found out he could come with Darian. *It's my fault.*

Then Darian wanted to walk to the exit, but he remembered how hard it was to walk to the volcano. If he would walk out of this side, he might have to walk an even longer way, so instead he decided to go the way from which they came. *It's my fault.* As Darian walked back he didn't notice the other path, for all his thoughts were with Isgur. He remembered how he and

Isgur went together into the woods to train. When they first began to train, he couldn't even swing his sword properly. *It's my fault.* On the bridge Isgurs body got heavy. It was like a sign to Darian, to leave him here, but he had to give him a proper burial. *It's my fault.*

He couldn't remember how he was walking back. He only noticed how he was suddenly at the end of the cave. Darian breathed deeply, before he walked outside into the warm and thick air. On his way back Darian always stayed near the mountain chain, as the air wasn't so thick there. The ship of Captain Craver was still at the shore. Darian didn't know, if he should be glad or sad about this. The ship came closer and closer and his legs got easier and easier. It was hard for Darian to not stumble or to fall down.

Only a few steps were between Darian and the ship, as Lira came running down from the ship. Darian fell on his knees and slowly laid Isgurs corpse on the sandy ground. His eyes were still wet, as he looked at Isgur. Lira knelt down too, in tears she hugged Isgur, trying to bring him back, not accepting his fate. Darian looked up and saw the crew looking down at them,

Darian saw the sun reflect in their eyes. Darian looked down at Lira. Darian never saw her crying so much. He hugged her and he felt how she was powerless and they both felt the same emptiness in their hearts.

They spoke no words. They only mourned.

After some time has passed they transported Isgurs corpse onto the ship. Captain Craver invited Darian and Lira to his cabin. Together they drank some wine and talked about the recent events. Craver told what happened on the ship and Darian reflected on what happened inside of the temple. Lira was able to hold back her tears.

„So what will you do now, Darian?", asked Craver. His voice was soft and he spoke with all of his condolence.

„Once your ship reaches the harbor, we'll bury him, give him a proper funeral. Then I'll have to go to the next temple.", Darian looked at Craver, but he noticed Lira was looking at him.

„Don't you think, your adventure has become too dangerous for you? I mean you know how you came out of the two temples.", Craver was looking at Lira, as he hoped not to have played with her feelings with his last sentence.

„I have to. This man, Belric, is still out there and he is on his way to the next temple and who knows what he might find in the temple. No, I can't leave this competition, not now. Not after all I had to do."

„I understand you, but I don't realize why both of you are racing from one temple to the next temple. What do these temples keep, that both of you seek? Did you ever find something inside the temples?"

„No, neither of us found anything inside the temples, besides each other and the markings to the other temples."

„Then what is the purpose of your competition?"

„Belric believes in the legends told about these temples, how these temples hold riches for every man and manuscripts of the folk, who built those temples."

„And your purpose?"

„At first I wanted to see, if these temples truly exist, if the legends are true. Then after I've first encountered Belric and his men. I saw a danger in Belric, that he might plunder the temples, so I decided to stop him and I won't quit now."

Darian left Craver with these words. He drank his cup empty and left with Lira. Together they looked again at the sunset. Lira still had wet eyes. They haven't spoken any words to each other, since Darian and Isgur left the ship of Craver. Darian held Lira in his arms, keeping her close beside him. The sky was orange, Darian and Lira now truly saw the beauty of a sunset. The beauty of life.

Chapter 9

Return to the little things

It was three days after the funeral. The clouds cried on that day, just as Darian and Lira did. They buried him under a big apple tree, because Isgur loved apples. They thought this would be the place, where he wished to be buried. On a hill, where the sun would shine on, once she returns to the face of earth and vanishes in the horizon. It was a hard day for Darian and Lira, it was just as the day that Isgur died in the temple. He went together with her to her home and the next morning he had to leave her. He rode across the border of the realm of the dwarves half a day ago. The clouds were grey and so was his mind, all what he could think about was Isgur and Lira, who he had to leave behind. Now in the darkest time, but if he waited one more day Belric might already be on his way to the next temple and Darian used the time, while he was on the boat with Lira, as best as he could. He felt a sudden cold crawling up his body. His horse was the same horse Darian bought in Landriel. It still hasn't got a name, but Darian thought about the name for many times throughout his journey.

He was riding in the mountains since he crossed the border of the realm. Nearly the whole realm of the dwarves is a single huge mountain chain. Only on region doesn't have any mountains and this is the Plane Island in the east of the realm. There are stories about how this is the only region without any mountains. One of them is that an ancient folk once lived there. This folk would've lived in the mountains, not like the dwarves nowadays do, but way deeper into the mountains. During the day they would go into their deep mines and mine there for rare minerals. They were once one of the wealthiest folks in this land, due to their rare materials, which they would sell in the biggest markets of the world. But their grief may have brought them to their doom. One day an earthquake occurred and due to their deep mines, the mountains didn't have any hold anymore and collapsed. Burying the cities and mines of this folk and with them their grief and their rare materials. It is even said the mountains around the Plane Island still have the mines and homes of this ancient folk. The legend doesn't give this folk a specific name, however the dwarves count this legend as a folk lore and they call this folk *the Rudnik*. But no one knows, if they truly existed and if they were the origin of the Plane Island.

On the mountain path were many trees and bushes on the right side. This way must be used very often, for the path is solid and not a dusty path, unlike the path Darian took when he rode to the very first temple. When he looked down into the vale he often saw a dwarven shepherd, with his sheeps and cows. The path led to the great city of the dwarven realm Krenn-so-ul, but Darian wasn't riding for Krenn-so-ul. Instead he wanted to ride far into the north, to the northernmost place of the dwarven realm and then he will go even further into the north. Where the sea is frozen and spikes hang down from the trees. It's even believed, that on some parts of the island, it isn't snowing, but spikes fall down from the clouds. Before he would go to the island, Darian definitely had to buy some furs to keep him warm.

Darian found the island, on which the next temple is hidden, while they were on their way back to the Black Harbor. He found it in the book, which he got, before he reunited with Lira and Isgur. Isgur took the book with him on their journey to the temples.

Cold crawled up his body again, as he reminded himself about Isgur and Darian started to think about something else. ‚I have to ride faster now or I'll have to sleep out in the cold again. I could make it to Quer-si-lo, before the darkness fills the world with coldness.', but he already felt the cold in his body. Darian looked into the sky and he only saw the grey clouds above him, but he guessed the sun would start to move towards the horizon. While he was thinking his horse started to trot faster.

His injuries from the last two temples healed perfectly. There was nearly no pain coming from his wounds anymore. Suddenly Darian was completely lost in his thoughts. ‚What am I actually doing here? Why am I on my way to the next temple, where again bad things could happen? Shouldn't I be with Lira and mourn with her? Could she ever forgive me? Of course not! First I was responsible for her greatest loss and now I just left her within the darkest time, she had ever known. I'm not with her. I'm not helping her. I'm not mourning with her. I'm not, where I'm supposed to be. Should I actually be alive at all? Horas should've rather killed me, than Isgur. I killed Horas, I avenged Isgur. But did it bring him back? *No and it's my fault.'*

As Darian rode on, he came across a cave, on the right side of the way and out of the cave came three dwarves. All of them were covered in dirt and sweat and they were surprised to see a man within the realm of dwarves. „Good day, traveler! May I ask, what brings a traveler like you, to a region like this?", said a dwarf with three grey strands coming from his chin. His old eyes studied Darians look.

„I have friends in this region or to be precise: In the north. I'm traveling to the town, which holds the name of Quer-si-lo. You must come from the great city of Krenn-so-ul?"

„No, not really. We come from a small settlement north of this cave. Our settlement is lesser known, for we don't have any special materials or herbs or anything special in general. We are only a small settlement in this far reaching country.", he had a bright smile on his face, which spread onto the two other dwarves and Darian too.

„From the looks of you, I presume a traveler could find hospitality in your settlement?"

„You can find as much hospitality, as you need! It isn't so far from here. Would you mind to come with us and sleep in our beautiful settlement, although your intended destiny is far away from it?"

„For surely, I will.", Darian dismounted his horse, took it by it's rein and further on he walked with the three dwarves. He helped one of them onto Darians horse, as he was exhausted by his work in the mine. They exchanged their names. The one with the grey strands is Bori. The other two are Dusty and Brocks. They told him Dusty and Brocks are siblings and Bori is their father. „Each family in our settlement is responsible for one specific necessity. Our family is responsible for all the ores and materials, which we need to build more lodgings or to keep our houses warm.", explained Bori.

„Do all small settlements do this?"

„We don't know, for we don't visit other settlements. We only know, that in greater cities like Krenn-so-ul or An-dro-sil it isn't like this. Within these cities everyone is independent from each other. In ours we are depending on our friends."

„It seems as if you don't have a hard life."

„No, it isn't hard, it's just a life full of duties and responsibility. But it is a nice life. Every time I'm walking along this path, it feels like I've never been here before. Then I have a feeling of deliverance of my duties. How about you? What is your life like Darian?"

Darian paused for a moment, „I cannot describe it. It's complicated, but I can say you this: It's a life I never could've imagined. Just as you have said it, it's a good life I have. But sometimes I'm asking myself, what if I would've taken another way? What if I decided to become a soldier or a farmer?"

„I know your thoughts. I had the same too, but once you realize the merriness of your life and the wealth, which waits in the future, you wouldn't wish any other life.", they smiled again.

„Is anyone of your people away to fight in the war?", Darian asked them with a very low voice.

„War? What war? There was no war for four year or so! What do you mean with this?", Bori looked with wonder and disbelief at Darian.

„Don't you know the news? Your folk is at war with the elves. The war rages in the east of your realm."

„Nay! We don't know anything about it! What ill news have gathered there in our realm? We only noticed, how some soldiers came riding down this path here, two months ago. But we only thought they were after some special carriage or something. We don't travel far away from our settlement, thus we don't know about anything what happens outside of our settlement!", they remained in silence for a moment, but soon started to talk again.

The path went on and on and it took them some time, until they reached the settlement. The settlement was built in a huge half circle of mountains and it was divided from the path with a fence. Four buildings were standing on the hillside of the mountains. With two more standing on a flat level, the buildings formed a circle and in the middle of the circle was a bigger house. All around the settlement were chickens walking around.

There was even a small plantation with cabbage, carrots and tomatoes. Darian could also see apple trees standing in the settlement. „This is our settlement and the building there in the middle is our longhouse. We are very proud of it, took us forever to build. In there we eat together, meet each other and talk about what has to be done in our settlement. But it also functions as a warehouse.", explained Bori to him, „You can leave your horse here by the water trough. It can rest there for the night and we'll bring her something to eat too.", so Darian bound the reins together with the fence and left his horse. „We also have some cows, sheeps and even some *Quarils*! But they're down in the valley. Our shepherd wanders everyday down into the valley and in the evening he comes back home, just as my sons and I do. Only that we walk to the mine and not down into the valley."

Four other dwarves greeted them and looked strange at Darian. „Don't mind their oblique faces, they aren't used to faces like yours.", they walked on. The house of Bori and his family was one of the houses, which are built at the hillside of the mountain. A small wooden staircase led to the entrance of the building. The wood creaked under the feet of Darian, it wasn't made for man. The house was small, so Darian had to duck, not to butt against the ceiling. The house was pleasant, with a chimney and a round table on which candles stood. The wall was grey and empty, only a pickaxe was hanging on it. The dwarves laid down their pickaxes. Brocks brought the bag with the ores to the longhouse.

„We have a spare bed, where you could sleep for the night. How long will you stay with us, Darian?"

„Only this night. Tomorrow in the morning I have to leave you, as I'm in a hurry."

„Pity, nonetheless we shall make this evening a festive one! Dusty! Tell the other families, that they shall prepare a feast! The Frigers shall prepare their biggest pig and they shall spice it with the best wort the Aligers have! Also the Tirtus shall go down into their brewery cellar, take their best met and fill our biggest jugs with them!", with this Dusty sprinted out of the house, „and while they're preparing everything. We will bring some wood to the chimney in the longhouse and make a fine fire, so we have it warm and cozy!"

„Bori, I'm speechless. You didn't have to do this. I would have been satisfied, with a simple dinner and a bed under a ceiling, but a feast? This is too much for a simple man like me."

„No, no it isn't! For such a guest, as you Darian, nothing is too much! We do not have many guests or travelers coming to our settlement and especially not travelers like you Darian!", this made Darian uncomfortable, for he wasn't prepared for such hospitality. But now it was too late for them to stop the preparations. It would disappoint the dwarves of the settlement.

As they got out, they saw everyone in a hurry. Going inside and outside of the longhouse and their homes. They walked to the back of the longhouse, where their storage was. The door was huge, even for Darian. Bori opened the door and in front of them was a large orderly room. On one side was the wooden material and on the other the ores, in the middle was the food and their wines.

It took them only a short manner of time to prepare everything, but at last the table of the longhouse was filled with meat of the pig, grilled tomatoes, salad with carrots, potatoes, and cucumber. There was also cheese and bread and the huge jugs were filled with met. Everyone was sitting at the round table and talked with the ones sitting next to them. They laughed and some spitted their food out of their mouth. It was a senseless company, but it was a cheerful one. For Darian there wasn't any temples anymore. No Belric. He didn't even think about Isgur. His heart was full of happiness and his thoughts were the best he had for the last four days.

„Ho Darian! Your jug is empty, here take some more met!", said Bori, who already had his third or fourth jug. Darian laid his hand on top of his jug.

„No, thank you I think I had enough.", Bori looked at Darian, on his face was the expression of confusion.

„Are you ill? Or don't you like the met?"

„No, you're met is the best one I ever had! I'm simply a man who doesn't drink so much, as you do. A single jug is enough for me."

„Well, then I'm relieved! Can I give you something else?"

„A little bit of the pig and some salad!"

„Here Darian! I already got it prepared!", said Brocks, who sat next to Darian. In his bushy grey beard were breadcrumbs and gravy of the pig. So this evening went on. Stories were told and jokes were made. Jugs were emptied and filled again. Songs were sung, together in a disordered choir and friendships were bound.

After the feast they were all tired and soon they all left the longhouse and went to sleep in their houses. Darian wasn't the last one, who left. Actually he was one of the first to leave them, as he had a long day ahead and needed some rest. Once he came out of the longhouse the stars greeted him. The clouds vanished and the stars shone bright in the dim moonlight. His horse was already sleeping. Together with Bori he went up the stairs to his house. Bori laid some furs on the warm ground. Darian laid down on the furs and closed his eyes. He was so tired it didn't take so long until his mind was in the world of dreams.

He returned to his dream of the darkness. There was still the brighter thing in the distance. As Darian walked slowly into its direction, it got bigger and brighter. Suddenly light overthrew the darkness and the darkness disappeared from the earth. The light blended him and he held his hand in front of his face. Then Darian was alone. In front of him was a mountain leading up into the clouds and a white horse standing next to him. He mounted the horse and started to ride along the mountain path. He rode to the top of the mountain, where a big lodge was standing. Once he reached it, he saw the sunset in the west. He dismounted his horse and admired the view. From the inside of the house came child laughter. Darian turned around and the door opened, through it came Lira and two little kids. Two sweet girls with dark hair. The kids sprang into the arms of Darian. Their voices cried out a word, *father*. Darians eyes got wet out of happiness. He smiled at the two girls and then at Lira, she was looking at the sunset, but she had a bright smile on her face. „I think for both you it's bedtime, isn't it?", Darian said to the girls. Lira turned to them and agreed. The girls fought at first with Darian, who was walking to the lodge. But at last they only laughed and then they entered the lodge.

Darian woke up with the singing of the birds. He looked around the room and saw how the sun shone through the small windows. Darian stood up and searched for Bori, but he couldn't find him. So he took his gear and walked to the longhouse. In the longhouse was a single plate and on it was a piece of bread with cheese and smoked ham, also there was an apple and a carrot. His jug was filled with milk. Next to the plate was a small note: *For Darian.* He sat down at the table and ate his breakfast. He spared the carrot for his horse. Suddenly the door opened and through it came Bori with his pickaxe on his shoulders. „Darian! How pleasant to see you here! I thought you were already gone!"

„And I thought you were already on your way to the mine. But as it seems your right about to leave."

„Right you are. Now Darian it was a pleasure meeting you and I sincerely hope we'll see each other again sometime."

„We will, I promise. Once I'm free of my duties. I shall visit your lovely settlement again."

„Then I wish you a farewell! Go with ease and may your road ahead be peaceful! Farewell!"

„Farewell, Bori!", and so Bori left the longhouse. Darian finished his breakfast and went out of the longhouse. He walked to his horse and unbound it from the fence. He mounted his horse and rode out of the settlement. He turned right and rode further north. Just after some moments he came to a crossing, the path to the left led to the mountain valley and the one to the right led to Krenn-so-ul. But Darian took the one in front of him, as this was the only path, which led to the north. Darian kicked into the flanks of his horse, so it would sprint now.

The path was very long, to Darian it seemed like this path would go on forever and he thought he would never reach the port in the north. But at last he saw the first glimpse of snow on the path and on the mountainside next to him. To his left side was a mountain sticking out, so that Darian couldn't see the vale anymore. After some time Darian saw a tower on the left side of the path. It was manned with two dwarves in a silver armor. Once they saw Darian, they pointed their arrows at him. „You, there riding along the path. Who are you and what are you doing here?", a dwarf with a smoky voice shouted at Darian.

„I'm Darian. I come from the realm of man."

„We are aware of this, we aren't blind."

„I'm just a traveler on my way to the north of your lovely country. What are you guarding here?"

„The city that goes by the name of Quer-si-lo."

„Didn't knew travelers are questioned, just because they are riding on a path, which leads past a city."

„These are war times we live in and we got orders to question every living thing, that isn't a dwarf or people, who look very suspicious to us. You aren't a dwarf and with your sword on your back, you are very suspicious to us."

„Calm down. I mean you no harm. Just as I've said I'm only traveling into the north. The sword on my back is for my own protection. You never know what lingers in this world."

„Alright, then go your way, traveler!", Darian nodded and rode on. As he was past the tower, he could see the city of Quer-si-lo emerging in the vale. Many houses were built into the mountains and a market was situated in the center of the city. Sparely he could see some dwarves walking on the market. There was a huge crowd around a podium or was it a fallen pillar? Darian wasn't sure. The city had many small streets, however it was less structured as other cities, the city looked more like the play room of two kids. On the stone roofs of the houses was some snow, due to the snow the city looked a bit magical. When he looked to the other side he saw some shepherds with their animals. As Darian looked back to the path ahead, he saw a caravan in front of him. It was a small carriage pulled by a young *Quaril*. On the carriage were four barrels loaded and the dwarf holding the reins looked exhausted and tired. Suddenly it began to snow. Snowflakes entangled in Darians hair and the hair of his horse.

Soon his ears started to hurt and his hands started to freeze, although he had gloves covering his hands. The hair of his companion wasn't brown anymore, but now it was white. To forget about the cold and the pain Darian started to remember a little story from his childhood.

Broken and fallen he stood on the hill,
His arms were thin and barren
His legs were thick and ailing,
Soon he shall fall, alone and broken.

But the hard times were still to come,
The cold bitted everywhere,
Spikes hung down from his arms,
All alone and soon to fall.

But hope was not lost for him,
New fellows came to him,
Remembered him of happy times,
For soon these times would return.

Renewed and robust he stood on the hill,
His arms regained their beauty,
His legs regained their strength,
Foul times are over, hopeful have
arrived.

Darian learned this story, when he was about to turn fourteen. His mother told it to him, when he was broken and he retold it very often, to remind him of the happier times. The cold returned to his mind and the road ahead of him still went on for some time and the snow wouldn't stop falling. But Darian tried to see the beauty in the snow. He looked up to the top of the mountains, covered in snow. When he looked down to the vale, he saw the traces of avalanches. Though they're dangerous, one simply cannot deny their beauty.

The sun was already starting her way to the horizon. The path went on and on and Darian was slowly tired of riding along this path. His horse started to stumble and Darian felt how they both were tired. His eyes were about to fall down, then he heard the sound of a seagull. Relief and hope came to his heart again. If he remembered right, there was no lake within the realm of the dwarves. The path turned right and behind the turn was the harbor town Ziral-se-ri. The town was smaller than Quer-si-lo, but bigger than the settlement where Bori lived. The seagulls were flying over the town. The town was completely covered in snow and ice spikes were hanging from the roofs. Suddenly the cold took completely over him.

Chapter 10

Biting Cold

Just like the dwarven realm was covered with mountains, the whole island was covered in snow. Mountains, hills and trees all were in the same color. Although he was covered in furs, he could still feel the bite of the cold. He couldn't feel both his hands nor his lips. It was so cold, even the snow was sometimes frozen and Darian was about to slip away. There were three mountains in front of him and in one of them the next temple must be hidden. Before the mountains was a small forest, where Darian had to walk through. But first he had to know, to which mountain he should walk. He observed the mountains, maybe he could see Belric and his men. They must be somewhere here on the island, as the seller of the boat crossing told him, how ten men payed a crossing. „It's rare to greet man in our town, but it's seldom to see them pay for a crossing to the islands.".

Somewhere Darian thought. He had to shut his eyes, the cold was to harsh and the snow was still falling. Before Darian got on his boat the seller warned him of the pain, which he would feel on these islands. But nothing could've fully explained how hard and dangerous it truly was. He looked down to the ground, where he suddenly saw some traces in the snow. There were many footsteps and they led into the forest.

Snow came falling down from the tree branches. The huge mass of snow nearly fell on his head and it would've buried him. His legs got weary. Darian didn't got much rest on the ship, for it wasn't a long crossing. But he did have enough time to talk with some crew members. Unlike the crew members of Captain Craver, these weren't as talkative. But some did at last speak with Darian, about the town of Ziral-se-ri. For example, that the town has a yearly parade. During the parade the dwarves would be dressed in the oddest ways, but together they formed a large crowd coming together out of reasons beyond thought. Most just say they attend the parade, because it's a tradition, but Darian thinks there is another reason: the sense of community and cheerfulness. The parade of the town remembered Darian of an event during his youth. It was a time, when Darian and Wilur visited a parade in the realm of the elves. The elven king traveled through most of the elven towns, but it wasn't the current king Honlarius, but the king before him, who attended the parade, due to his current coronation. They were in the elven city of Gomadriel and Darian was still a young man. Darian was standing in the front line of the bystanders. Once the king came riding by, Darian looked at him with a stunned face, for he has never seen an elven king before with all his glory and strength. Suddenly the king turned to Darians side and looked right at him. He waved and smiled at him. Darian still had a stunned face and only realized what just happened after the king already rode out of sight. The look of the king bewitched Darian, but it was an event, which Darian would never forget.

Slowly he realized how he was so absorbed in his memories, that he didn't noticed how far he already was into the forest. He even forgot about the pain of the cold for a moment, but it came back as soon as he was back in the present. Then Darian saw something black in the snow. He had a guess and this guess became a fact, as he got closer. Belric only got eight men left and Darian had to be quick or he might meet them within the forest.

The trace went to the eastern mountain. Darian kept following the path. As he got to greater heights, he walked more carefully and he nearly fell down a cliff, as his feet slipped away due to the ice. His feet gave up and he had to rest for a moment, but Darian used this moment to turn around and look at the island, from a high ground. It was astonishing for him, to see an island covered completely in snow. The whole island looked like one mighty mass. Suddenly he felt like someone was looking at him from behind, so he turned around and saw Lira standing behind him. Her dark hair stood out from the snow. Lira was like a glimpse of light in the darkness. She bowed forward and kissed his forehead and then she vanished again. Darian felt new energy in his legs and stood up again. He followed the trace, along the hillside of the mountain, where trees were standing on small stone platforms. Soon he stood before a great entrance. The entrance was a great arc out of ice and symbols were carved into the ice. When he looked beyond the entrance Darian saw walls out of ice and the ground looked like ice too. Slowly

Darian walked through the entrance and once he stood beyond the entrance relief felt upon him, for the ground wasn't as slippery as Darian thought it would be.

Slowly he walked through a narrow path, on the icy walls were further symbols. He was inside the temple. As he walked on, the cold crawled underneath his furs. The path divided into two paths, each one in a separate direction. There were noises, talking noises. Darian waited to realize from where the noises would come. He guessed the voices came from the right, so Darian chose the left path.

The path turned slowly to the right. The voices could still be heard. There was an angry voice shouting, but also calm voices. The angry voice must be the one of Belric.

„Everybody, stop talking!", the angry voice shouted through the whole temple, „What was that noise?", the voice came again. Darian stood still and held his breath. Tension was in every muscle of his body. His hand slowly moved to his sword, prepared to grab it once Belric and his men spotted him. Then there were loud screams coming from both directions. Darian decided to go on. *Maybe someone woke the upholder of this temple. If it's true, then I have to be quick or I shall find my death in here.*

The path divided again, one path led onward and the other turned to the right. He looked into the sideway, but he could only see the ice of the walls. So he decided to walk onward. Soon Darian stood before a slope to an ice hall. On the opposite side of the hall was a path and on the left side of the hall were four persons. Two of them were standing with their backs at the wall and the remaining two had their weapons drawn and pushed the other two against the wall. But the two armed persons had strange weapons and a strange look. Their armor had an ice blue look, just like their weapons.

Darian jumped down the slope and looked at the armed persons. They turned around and they looked extraordinary. Darian couldn't see their faces, behind their armor they looked more like creatures, than human beings. Darian slowly walked at the creatures and while walking he drew his sword. The creatures prepared for Darians attack. Darian pushed through them and blocked their attacks. Their swords clashed and oddly the sound of steel hitting ice resounded.

Darian now stood before the two other persons. „Stay behind me, you understand?", Darian said to the two men. The creatures turned around and attacked Darian. Darian parried their attacks and swung his sword to both directions. He kicked to his side and swung his sword above his head down to one creature. His sword hit the creature at the hip, but the sword only hit the armor. Darian pushed the creature away and turned around to the other creature. He attacked from below to break the defense of the creature and it worked. Next he placed his sword at his side and slit it against the creature. A strange noise came from the creature and on Darians sword was ice. Out of the wound of the creature came smoke.

The other creature stood up again and attacked Darian. Darian countered the attacks, with a strike from above and from the side and to finish he stabbed it with his sword through the creatures belly. He pulled his sword out of it and again his sword had an icy look on it. Both creatures now made the strange noises. At last they lay on the ground, motionless.

Darian turned to the two men, they watched the whole fight and didn't move. They had swords at their hips and wore big furs around their shoulders like Darian. Both of them were very thin. „Thank you very much!", they said to Darian.

„What are these things?", he asked them.

„We don't know, we only searched here for markings on the wall and then suddenly these things attacked us.", one of them pointed at one of the dead creatures.

„Where are the other men of your company?"

„Somewhere behind this path. Also searching for markings and for gold or riches.", the other one pointed at the path on the opposite side of the hall. Darian walked to the wall and saw how on the wall were markings carved into the ice. There was a long, irregular line with a turn in it. Next to the line was a cross. *The cross must be the next temple*, Darian thought. But what did the line mean? Darian thought about it for some time. The other two men were on the opposite wall and searched there for markings. Suddenly it came to Darians mind. The line could represent the great river of Emlir. Darian searched in a bag at his hip. In it he found the book of old Greg and it immediately brought ill memories back. In it he searched for a map of the known world. Once he found it he realized, what the markings resemble. The next temple is situated near the great river of Emlir. The cross must be in the realm of elves. The two men walked to Darian, they noticed how he was watching at the wall and then they saw the markings, too.

Darian fell to the ground, as a quake occurred. He stood up fast, with the help of his sword and again he felt some energy going through his body. Then the two men and Darian walked to the path through which they wanted to leave the hall, when suddenly the icy ground of the hall broke and fell down into the unknown. All three turned around and looked at the ground. Something came out of the broken ground and grabbed the remaining ice ground. The thing looked like an arm and Darian knew what was about to show itself. The hand pushed a whole body out of the broken ground and in the hall now stood the upholder of the temple. Just like the temple, the giant was made out of ice. The two men were still standing next to Darian. But once the giant turned around and looked at Darian with it's blue eyes, they started to run away.

Though Darian had a moment to think about the markings, his body was still full of tension. Almost as if his body knew about the looming thread underneath the ground. The path took a turn to the right and immediately separated into two paths. Darian followed the path onward and didn't turn to the left. Then Darian saw another icy creature standing in the path. Darian turned himself and his sword around and clashed it against the creature. The creature fell dead to the ground and Darian ran onward, nearly stumbling. The path led to a smaller hall and in the hall many men were standing around, men of Belric. Now Darian was running even faster to get as far away as possible from the host.

Darian came to the first separation of the temple, so he turned left to the entrance of the temple. Where another creature was standing, which was about to attack Darian from above. He blocked the attack and with one blow he attacked the spiky legs of the creature. The creature fell down and Darian ran out of the temple.

Snow was falling into Darians face and from behind he heard many steps coming near to him. Darian walked on, until he fell down the hillside. He was rolling through the snow, down the hillside. Some trees passed him and he was still rolling.

Darian had to stop or he would be lying dead at the end of the mountain. Suddenly something stopped Darian from rolling further. He started to feel pain at his forehead. His fur and his hair was full of snow. As he looked up he realized something red in the snow. He touched his forehead with his hand, then he looked at his hand. His glove was slightly red, but it wasn't as much as Darian expected.

Then he looked at the entrance of the temple again. He could see how the host was coming out of the temple. Then he heard some voices coming from above. Darian didn't move, trying to stay hidden from the greedy eyes of Belric and his men. Among them were the two men, who Darian rescued in the hall. They started to walk down the path. Darian kept lying in the snow, until Belric and his men were in the forest. Then he slowly stood up and walked down the hillside. Sometimes he fell, due to the snow and he skidded down the hillside a bit.

Once Darian reached the end of the hillside, he took a deep breath and looked around him. The forest was to his left and to his right was the coast of the island. The mountain leaped over the coast and Darian saw a frozen waterfall running down into the ocean. Darian stared at the waterfall with astonishment. Again and again the nature proves what a beauty it actually is. Even in such a forsaken place.

The cold returned and with it the pain of his forehead returned. He wagered on where to go now. Suddenly it came to his mind. *How am I supposed to get off this island?* Belric and his men are probably taking the crossing to the town of Ziral-se-ri. Darian didn't know when the next crossing would arrive and he couldn't survive very long in this cold region without any heat or food. He might have firestones with him, but there wouldn't be any dry wood to be found on this island and his torches were, after his fall from the hillside, wet too. Darian wasn't able to make a fire, so he had to find a way to get off this island fast.

Darian couldn't see Belric nor his men in the forest. They might already be of the island. Slowly he walked through the forest, he found the footsteps of Belric and his men in the snow. Sometimes there were red dots in the snow. The footsteps led through the forest, to the shore. Darian followed them and soon found a puddle of red snow next to a tree. One of the men probably got hurt by one of the creatures.

The grey clouds were still roaming in the sky. The snow was still falling on the ground. The cold still hurt Darians face and hands. The sun started to sink and thus the darkness slowly crept on the shores of the island and the darkness was about to fill the world and the darkness aided the cold. Darian was now at the shore, looking for boats, which could bring him back to the realm of dwarves again.

Although there are crossings to the Icelands. The islands don't count to the realm of dwarves, due to the lack of usage of these islands. All of the time these islands are captured in snow, ice and cold. So they aren't fruitful or even habitable. Rumors say, that on the Icelands people are living in round ice caves and they've got a mysterious way of keeping themselves and their homes warm, but as it is with most rumors: no one knows if they are true.

However for Darian it was unbelievable to stay alive under such conditions. His legs were weak and he couldn't feel his face anymore. The land became darker and darker with every minute passing. He looked across the ocean and searched for ships, which might be passing this island. Slowly he turned around and looked at the island and it's mountains again. Ill thoughts filled his mind and he couldn't do anything but to think about them. He turned to the ocean again and saw Lira standing next to him. She was grabbing his arm and she laid her head on his shoulder. Together they watched at the ocean and wondered what would behind the horizon for them.

Darian closed his eyes, his heart was now uplifted with Lira standing next to him, it all seemed so real for him. He couldn't even feel the cold anymore, but rather the warmth of Lira. However once he opened his eyes again, Lira vanished and the cold returned. *Why did I open my eyes?* He looked at the ocean and saw something moving on the ocean. He looked closely at this thing. It was something in a dark color and it had something sticking into the air. Was it a ship? Darian wasn't sure, so he decided to wave with his arms. Maybe just maybe these would be his saviors. The thing came even closer and slowly he realized: It truly was a ship. Darian waved with his hands again, as long as his strength allowed it to him. The ship came closer and closer. Relief filled his heart. Darian knelled down into the snow. His eyes kept on the ship. Darian laughed, he didn't notice the cold taking over him and in the next moment he was lying in the snow.

Chapter 11

The calm...

There was no cold anymore, instead he felt the warmth of a good fire again. Slowly his eyes opened and he stared at a stone ceiling. But it seemed to him, as if the ceiling was lower, than he was used to. He turned his head to the right side, where he looked at a stone wall. He turned his head to the left side, where he looked at a chimney. Before the chimney was a brown carpet. Next to the chimney was a small window, as he looked through it, he could only see a snowy hillside. He sat up and looked around the rest of the room. There was a small staircase leading upstairs and downstairs. There were some paintings on the wall. Besides the crackling of the wood, he heard voices coming from the outside and boots walking on wood. The door opened and in the door stood a dwarf, with long black hair and a long black beard. His eyes were grey and his eyes looked at

Darian. The dwarf was covered in furs and under the fur was a tunic. With a big smile he walked at Darian, while walking he took of his furs. Revealing the brown tunic with small green stripes around the sleeves. The dwarf laid the fur on a stone bank, standing next to Darians bed.

„I hope you have it warm and comfortable, after such a torture up on that island. Now what brings a man like you so far into the north of this world? Furthermore I find it interesting, that you went all alone, which usually is a judgement of death in such regions.", he sat down on the stone bank, waiting for an answer from Darian.

„I've heard stories about the islands and I wondered, if they're true. So I decided to travel to the island, explore them and find out if the stories tell the truth."

„And bold deadly creatures were mentioned in the stories, so you needed something to defend yourself. This would be your explanation for bringing a sword with you, right?", suddenly a shock shot through Darians mind. *Where is my sword? Did he take it? I can't see it within this room.* „But I wouldn't be satisfied with this explanation. Cause your sword isn't made out of common steel. Just as the hilt of it. I've never seen such a sword before, where did you get it?"

„It's a gift and I will not say from whom, as it isn't to your concern. I hope you understand me. Nonetheless I'm grateful that you rescued me, from the island and I thank you very deeply.", the dwarf smiled. Darian noticed small golden rings at the ears of the dwarf and it was an unusual look for Darian. Not every dwarf can buy such things, the same goes for the tunic of the dwarf. *Who is he?*

„Do you feel powerful enough to settle your horse and go riding again?", with sharp eyes he looked at Darian. Darian wasn't sure what he should say. He didn't even now in what a situation he is right now nor who his savior actually is.

„I think I am."

„Good, we'll leave shortly. You've got enough time to prepare your belongings.", the dwarf smiled and walked outside.

„Wait! Where are we going to ride?"

„South.", the dwarf picked up his furs and left Darian with this word in the room. Darian stood up and searched for his belongings. His sword was leaning to the chimney and his furs were lying next to the chimney. He swung his sword and his other belongings to his back and fastened it together with his belts. He placed his furs around his shoulders, the brown fur scratched Darians neck. He warmed his hands at the chimney and then he walked outside. He was standing in a small place, surrounded by small stone houses. Everything was covered in snow. In the center of the place were six dwarves sitting on *Quarils*. There was another, yet unmounted *Quaril*. The dwarves wore silver armor and had short swords on their hips and their *Quarils* had shields on their sides. Next to the *Quarils* Darians horse was standing, already settled.

Darian walked to his horse and mounted it. He looked into the faces of his next company. They all had faces of steel, no emotion not even a glimpse of it. Then he looked around the place. There was a small tavern and a fur shop. Slowly Darian recognized the place. The fur shop was the shop, from which Darian bought his furs.

„Is everyone ready to leave?", the voice came from the small tavern. The armored dwarves shouted in a collectively sound. The voice came from the dwarf, who first met Darian.

„Good to hear lads!", the dwarf laughed and mounted the remaining *Quaril*. The dwarf had his thick furs on his shoulders again. Now he looked to Darian. „The question was also meant for you.", Darian nodded, „Good, then lets go.". The dwarf kicked into the flanks of the *Quaril* and it started to walk. Darian rode next to him, before them were two armored dwarves and behind them were the remaining four. Together they left the town, through the south-western mountain path, the same one which Darian rode when he first came to the town.

There were only few dwarves outside, as it's still early in the morning and as dwarves are a very sleepy folk. The streets of every town and settlement will be empty to this time, except for guards or merchants. During such times most carriages loaded with food or herbs arrive in the dwarven towns.

„So tell me, what is the meaning of you taking me, a complete stranger to you, with you for a ride to the south?", Darian looked at the dwarf next to him.

The dwarf sighed „There always has to be a meaning for everything right? Can't it just be a friendly request to join someone for a ride, share stories and eventually become close friends?"

„Usually I won't say anything against such a venture, but I admit it's suspicious to me, when the company I'm traveling with consists of six armed guards."

„Oh don't worry about them, they're simply here for our protection. Just as your own sword is.", the dwarf smiled at Darian with a trustworthy face. Meanwhile the company was already high up in the mountain path.

„I have a question, about you.", the dwarf looked at Darian with a curious face, „What was your duty up in the north? I mean it's a rarity to see six dwarven guards, together with a wealthy dwarf to sail around the most northern parts of our world."

„How do you want to know, that I'm a wealthy dwarf?"

„You wear clothes only few dwarves are able to afford and even if you had just enough gold to buy such clothes, why would six soldiers follow your orders?"

„Well your assumption is partly true. Yes I am a wealthy dwarf, but these dwarves are not mine. They only fulfill their duty. You have to know, that I'm a cartographer and in the order of my king I was supposed to investigate the northern islands and to gather informations about them, so that I can draw maps of these islands."

„And now you're on your way to represent your results to your king, right?"

„Right and I must say, he will be very pleased with these results.", now they remained in silence and enjoyed the breathtaking landscape of the mountains. The journey to the south passed quicker, then the journey to the north, as they were already on the road to Krenn-so-ul. Every time Darian travels together with someone else, the time flies by for him, but once he travels alone it seems to him, as if he wouldn't be moving at all. He didn't even realize, that they already passed the town of Quer-si-lo. The first travelers could be seen on the road, besides the merchants.

„Will you follow us into the great city of Krenn-so-ul? I could recommend you a tavern with the best ale our realm has to offer or a smith, who forges you the best sword you could ever imagine, for a relatively small amount of gold.", the dwarves voice was full of excitement.

„No I have to disappoint you. I won't be able to stay so long in the city. I'll have to ride on, as soon as we arrive the city. But I'll remember your recommendations and I shall visit them, once I have more time."

„But where do you have to go, that you're in such a hurry?", his face changed from excitement to disappointment.

„I heard about some legends in the south and they grabbed my attention and I have a feeling, I'm not the only one, who is going after this legend. But it's very important, that I'm the first one, who discovers the truth about this legend. Nonetheless I'm willing to come with you at least until we've reached the city gates."

„Fine and then I shall tell you my recommendations.", the dwarves face was happy and Darian felt good again. The road got broader, which indicates that a city is nigh. Snow was lying here on the ground too, but the snow wasn't falling from the sky anymore.

The first watchtower appeared, behind the hillside of a mountain. In the tower were three guards armed with bow and arrow. Slowly the great city of Krenn-so-ul emerged, with its thousands of buildings. Just as the settlement of Bori, the city of Krenn-so-ul was built within a half circle of mountains, but much bigger than the settlement of Bori. The city has three different layers. The first one is the poorest one. The second layer is situated on the hillside of the valley. Here the wealthy dwarves have their homes and the great market lays within the second layer. Within the third layer are the greatest buildings of Krenn-so-ul standing in the highest regions of this area, most stand on top of the mountains. First of all the great grand citadel, in which the great history of the dwarves is hidden. Thousands of books are sheltered there, all about the lore, the culture and the many wars of the dwarven folk. In it's great tower looming from the center are the most documents stored. When the city was once under siege, hundred soldiers guarded the great tower and rumors say, the elves had planes to lit the tower in flames. But to the relief of everyone, the elves had to quit the siege after only a short amount of time. This incident was three hundred years ago. Another building in the third layer is the memoriam of heroes. A great hall in which the greatest persons and warriors of the dwarven folk are buried. Everyone also has his own statue. The kids, who once visited the memoriam of heroes, all have one dream: To have a very own place in the memoriam of heroes. The kings palace however isn't standing in the third layer. Instead it's built around the second layer. The palace goes into the mountain and it's covered from the many houses of the dwarves.

As Darian looked up to the third layer, he only saw the silhouettes of the buildings. The company turned left, onto the road to the gate of Krenn-so-ul. Before the gates were some plantations. Dwarves were working on the plantations and merchants were leaving the city. Once a merchant was beyond the gate, the gate was immediately shut again. As they approached the gate more and more guards stood on the high wall. Darians eyes kept on the guards and the guards eyes kept on Darian.

„Who comes there?", asked one of the guards.

„Zari, a cartographer in the duty of our king.", said the dwarf next to Darian.

„I know, I asked your companion.", the eyes still stared at Darian. Darian smiled friendly.

„I am Darian. I come from the realm of man, as you can see. This dwarf here, saved me from certain death and he asked me to join him. I won't stay very long, to be precise you can actually leave the gate open. I will leave shortly.", then Darian and the guard exchanged a long look.

„Open the gate", the dwarf said. The other guards separated from each other and Darian and Zari rode through the gate. When Darian looked into the city, he could see a very long street filled with many dwarves and stands. On both sides were houses made out of stone. But one thing sprang into Darians eyes: A dwarf with rags, lying at the corner of a street. He was shivering, no wonder as the city was covered in snow too. His face was dirty and he had a look in his face, which hurt Darians heart.

Zari brought a map out of a bag, which was hanging at his *Quaril*. „Here on this map, I'll mark you the taverns and shops, I would recommend you to visit."

„No, mark your house on the map and once I come to this city again, I shall visit you at home and then you can show me everything, personally.", Zari crossed his house and then he gave the map to Darian. Darian stowed the map in his bag. He glanced at the dwarf in the corner again, then he dismounted his horse and walked to the dwarf. He was feeling how Zari stared at him. Darian removed his furs from his shoulders and gave them to the dwarf. „Here, they shall keep you warm.", said Darian to the dwarf. The dwarf replied with a quiet voice „Thank you, very much." and on his face was a glance of happiness and hope.

„Fare thee well!", he said in a soft voice to the dwarf. Darian walked back to his horse. Zari was waiting for him. „Why did you do this?", he looked confused, even a bit angry.

„What? Why I gave this poor fellow, something to keep him warm?"

„Yes, exactly. These furs would've been more useful for you, than for him. You could've at least asked him for something in return."

„No, they wouldn't. I'm riding south and I guess I can't return into the north so quickly and winter is coming. It will be hard for him, if he doesn't have anything to warm him. He doesn't have to give me anything in return, as he doesn't have anything to spare. If it's one thing that I learned during my many trips around this world then it would be this: The ones with the most to spare, are the most unlikely to share.", Darian mounted his horse.

„It's useless: This poor dwarf is one of thousands poor dwarves, let it alone be in this city.", Zari became unfriendly. It seemed as if he was insulted by Darian, but Darian just wanted to teach him a lesson on how to make other people and oneself merrier.

„Nonetheless he is one of them", replied Darian. The dwarven guards looked at Zari and they exchanged a look.

„My security calls for me, so I guess, this is a goodbye Darian."

„I wouldn't call it a goodbye. I'd prefer a farewell.",
Darian smiled at Zari.

„Then farewell, Darian."

„Farewell, Zari.", Darian bowed to him and then Zari started to ride into the crowds in the street. Darian left the city again and the gate was closed immediately. Darian slowly rode to the main street and turned to the left. On the street were many carriages on their way to the city and some just came out of the city. Once the city vanished behind the mountains Darian rode faster, as the race between Darian and Belric was in its final round. Darian was already in five temples, each one represented one element and since there are six elements, only one temple remained.

He started to feel guilty and bad and questioned himself if it was wrong what he said to Zari, if he was to harsh with him. But he had to say it, as it is an urgent problem within the realm of dwarves. No other realm has so many poor dwarves living on the street without any shelter. Darian already tried to convince wealthy dwarves to build buildings, in which the poor dwarves could live, eat and have a warm place. But no one realized this idea. Darian has been fighting against this problem, since the first time he travelled to Krenn-so-ul and he will still be fighting.

His thoughts returned to the temple. He thinks about, what might wait for him in the temple. But with the thoughts about the temples returned the thoughts about what could've been and what should'e never happened. *It's my fault.* The cold was crawling up to his mind again. Now he could only think about Lira and what he did to her, so he forgot about the time again. He even rode past Bori's settlement without notice. The sun started to sink already and the light vanished behind the mountains, but Darian didn't rest for this night, for now every minute is important for him. Also there wasn't any opportunity for Darian to stay for the night. He could've rode back to Krenn-so-ul, but the next day he would have to ride even longer and Belric might have already been in the temple. So he rode on and hoped to not feel exhausted, once he would reach the temple. Now he only hoped for a dry night and a fast journey.

The stars started to shine up high in the dark sky and they guided Darian through the night. He already crossed the great river of Emlir. He rode over the biggest bridge leading over the river outside of a city. There are bigger bridges, which lead through a city and these bridges are the most used bridges by merchants. The road went straight on, thus Darian occasionally glanced at the stars. He also looked at the two moons up high in the sky. One of them was light blue and the other one was light red. A story tells that the moons resemble the balance or the stability of this world. That there's alway an opposite. Light and Dark. Peace and War. Love and Hate. Life and Death. A prophecy tells how once there shall come a time, when one of the moons disappears and then either the bad things or the good things will remain in this world. The other side will disappear from this world, just like the moon.

Darian never knew what he should think about this prophecy, he never really liked prophecies. He is more interested in stories and legends. But Darian did believe, that the two moons have to represent something in their world, maybe they truly represent a balance and he also hoped how someday the bad things within this world would just drift away. *Hopefully*, he thought then he took a deep breath and closed his eyes.

Chapter 12

... before the storm

It was day again and the sun now had her mighty time and Darian wasn't tired. At the first glance of the sun, Darian reached the realm of elves. Darian was now about to cross the river of Emlir again, but this time within the realm of elves and then he would reach the temple before the dawn of the sun. Darian was glad to be back in the realm of elves. He wasn't in the realm, since he rode for the Dark Harbor. Due to the harshness of the dwarven realm and the darkness of the realm of man, he soon missed the calmness of the realm of elves. Especially after the recent events. In every corner of the forest were different kinds of animals wandering, lurking through the woods and observant travelers might see such an animal within their daily life. The birds were singing their hymn loudly into the forest, bringing the forest to life even more.

Darian also shares his merriest memories with the realm of elves. One memory is Darians first feeling of love for another person, besides his friends or parents. It was a sunny day in the realm of elves. During that time Darian was about 22 years old and he stayed in Morunsil, as he and Wilur were on their way to an old oasis of knowledge. Wilur decided to stay for some time in the city and Darian spent this time to learn the daily life in an elven city. Darian was on the market street and a merchant of the realm of man happened to need some help with his goods, so Darian helped him. While helping him he saw the daughter of the merchant. She had long chestnut-brown hair and it truly remembered Darian of a forest during the autumn. She also had some freckles on her face. He saw in front of him a beautiful, young woman. Though she was very shy, Darian did meet her on the same evening. As both of them had to leave the next day in different directions, they decided to spent the evening together. Together they watched the thousands of lights of an elven city and they got to know each other better. Darian can still remember how she never wanted to work as a farmer or a merchant, instead she wanted to do something different, but she couldn't explain what. Darian invited her to travel with him, however she had to go with her father back to the realm of man and thus they departed the next morning and never met each other again. Another memory would be his many days together with Wilur learning about the meaning of life.

On the road was a branch of a tree and the wood cracked once Darians horse walked over it. While thinking about his happy memories Darian didn't notice how he already crossed the river. He noticed it once an offspring river appeared next to Darian. Now Darian only had to follow the river into the south and then he would reach the last temple. Darian looked up to the tree branches. The branches were so dense, he couldn't see the sky, only some parts and these parts looked unfriendly. *So it shall rain*, he thought. The road wasn't out of gravel anymore, instead now it was the solid earth. The earth looked nearly untouched, only some footprints of horses could be seen. *Are these the footprints of the horses of Belric and his men?* Darian didn't hope this was the truth, but he could only hope.

Then there was a strange sound coming from above. It wasn't the sound of birds singing nor the sound of breaking branches. Then something fell on Darians nose. Darian looked up to the branches and then it came to his mind. It's raining and the sound was the rain falling onto the leaves of the trees. The whole forest was silent, there was only the sound of the rain falling down. The animals hid in their nests and watched the rain touching the ground. Before Darian was a small hill and from behind it came strange noises. A horse, a voice, another voice and another horse. Darian unmounted his horse and slowly walked to the top of the hill, then he laid down and watched beyond the hill. The forest would still go on for miles, but there was a hole in the ground and around the hole stood four men, one of them was Belric. He screamed at the three other men and pointed around the hole, then he walked down into the temple. Darian didn't recognize any of the men. All three men wore a hood. Two had a sword and a shield, the last one had a bow on his back.

Suddenly Darians horse startled. The three men looked to their horses, but they stood still, so they watched to Darians direction. One of them shouted: „Who's there? Come out or we'll have to use violence.". Darian slowly stood up and walked down the hill. Darians heart raced and his muscles are filled with tension. *Don't say anything wrong*, he reminded himself.

„He has a sword on his back.", said one of them.

„Maybe this is the one, Belric warned us about.", said another one. The man with the bow laid an arrow on his bow, pulled the string and pointed the tip of the arrow at Darian. Darian could now see into the faces of the three men, all of them had painful faces and fearful eyes.

„Hold. You don't want to do this and neither do I", said Darian to the three men. They watched at each other.

„How do you want to know about this?", said the man with the bow.

„Cause I know, what you've been through. Some time ago Belric came to you with an offer. That he will grant you with gold and riches, if you'd follow him on an expedition. You accepted the offer, as you have a family with one, two maybe even three children and you would do anything to grant them a good life. So you decided to come with Belric on his expedition to gain some gold and to provide your family with food. However he never told you what this expedition would ask you to do, that you would have to use a weapon, that you have a risk to die or to kill someone else. You are no men, who would kill to gain some gold. Otherwise you would serve the army of the king of man."

„How do you know this?", another man asked. The man with the bow lowered his hands slowly.

„As you've started this expedition you were about twenty men, now you are only three. Most of you died and some left your expedition. One of them was Erich. He was ordered to kill me in my sleep, but he failed. Also I can see your fear in your eyes.."

„Did you kill him?", the last one asked.

„No, I became friends with him. Now he should be with his family again and go after his regular work in a tavern.", the men exchanged looks amongst themselves.

„And now what? Do you think we'll just leave, without any gold?", asked the man with the bow.

„Go home, to your families and grant them with everything they deserve, for Belric won't find any gold or riches in this temple."

„Liar! There are! The legends tell about them! Otherwise how do you know about this?", shouted the man with the bow.

„Legends don't always tell the truth, that's why they're called legends. These temples don't hold riches or gold, but wisdom. Wisdom not even I am able to understand.", again they exchanged looks, „So I'm begging you. Leave this foul expedition and go to your families, they need you. Let me pass, so that I can explain everything to Belric.", slowly they dropped their weapons and mounted their horses.

„Fare thee well to our savior.", they said.

„A merry life for you and your families.", Darian smiled at them and they smiled back. Darian felt good and his heart felt good too. Now he prepared to face Belric. He looked down into the hole, he saw stairs leading down into darkness. He took a deep breath and started to walk down the stairs.

The walls became flat and the ground turned from rough earth to solid earth. Once and every while a crystal was hewn into the walls, from them came a light and so neither Darian nor Belric had to use any torches. Darian heard grumbling coming from the inside of the temple. He came to the last steps down into the temple. The path went straight on, seemingly into a hall. Before the path led into the hall, it departed into two more paths. When Darian came to the separation, he looked into both directions. Each of them turned into the direction of the hall. Darian decided to walk into the hall, as Belrics voice seemed to come from ahead. As he walked into the hall, he realized it wasn't so small as he expected it to be, instead it came to the size of the very first temple. The hall was even bigger, than the one of the very first temple Darian entered. The light crystals were hewn even to the ceiling of the hall. Belric was looking at the wall to the left of Darian. It seemed to Darian, as if he was searching for something. He hasn't noticed Darian yet.

He was swearing, „Where are the markings? Where is the gold, the riches? They've got to be somewhere here. There must be clues to the riches!"

„There are no more markings, as there are no more temples. We both are now within the last temple, that exists at least from this kind.", Belric startled and turned around. He quickly moved his hand to the handle, „And there is no gold nor riches to be found in these temples."

„Then what are these temples for, Darian? After all the time, all the fighting, all the losses, did we in the end hunt after nothing?", he smirked at Darian in such a way, that Darian had to control himself not to attack Belric right off. Perhaps this was the plan of Belric.

„No, at least I didn't. If you would become a wiser man and less a greedy one, then perhaps you haven't too. These temples don't keep treasures, with gold and riches beyond measure. Instead they keep wisdom, wisdom of an ancient folk, living way before the first humans."

„I don't seek for wisdom. But perhaps I could use this wisdom for my own benefit. There are some people in this world, which would pay a fine amount of gold for such wisdom or informations about this ancient folk.", again he smirked.

„Wisdom isn't something, that you can sell to people."

„You think so? Oh I could show you.", there was nothing, which bothered Darian more, then Belric and his greed. It bothered him how he stood there with his hands raised and his smirk on his face, which kind of never changed.

„I will prevent you from doing so.", Darian started to move his hand to the handle of his sword.

„So you want to end this now? I have a question, before we really end our journey. How did you come past my men? You didn't kill them, cause then you would have at least some wounds or I would've heard something. So tell me, Darian."

„I sent them away, back home to their families. I told them, the same thing I've said to you, that there won't be any treasures in this temple or any other temple. Then I convinced them this didn't have to end in a violent way and it didn't."

„Well then, Darian. Let's end this lovely journey of ours.", as Belric said these words he drew his sword and started to walked at Darian. Darian walked at Belric too and while walking he drew his sword from his back. Their swords clashed above their heads and then they clashed again underneath their stomachs. They turned around and their swords clashed again. Belric stroke right at Darians stomach, but Darian was able to dodge the strike. Then Belric swung his sword above his head and down at Darians head. Darian raised his sword against the sword of Belric. Next came a moment, where both of them were able to look into each others eyes before they returned to thrusting their swords at each other. The temple was filled with the noise of steel hitting steel. Both got exhausted very fast.

Once the distance between them increased, Belric started to talk. „You are fighting pretty well, I'll have to admit that.", in Belrics voice was exhaustion, „It's a shame such a talent will fade away by the end of this day.". Then they returned to fighting each other. Their swords clashed so many times, Darian didn't hear the sound of them hitting anymore. Suddenly Darian felt how behind him was a wall. Belric was pushing him to the wall and thus Darian would become an easy opponent. With his back to a wall he was vulnerable. Belric attacked from above, Darian rammed his shoulder to Belrics hip. Through this he escaped from the wall.

Their swords clashed above their heads again. Belric pushed Darians sword to the wall and Darian pushed Belrics sword aside again. Thus their swords swung from one side to the other. Darian whipped his sword alongside Belrics and attacked him from below, but Belric blocked and countered the attack. Both of them fell down and something rumbled inside the temple. Darian soon realized it was a quake and he knew what comes with a quake inside these temples. Suddenly he realized how his sword wasn't in his hands anymore. Belric was lying next to the wall and he was slowly standing up. Suddenly a wall on the other side of the hall collapsed and the wall crumbled down. Dust was coming from where once the wall stood. Slowly a stone giant came through the dust, in his hand was a long stone staff. Belric was already on his feet and running to an entrance of the hall. Darian was looking for his sword. He looked to his left and then to his right and there it was lying. He stretched his arm to grab his sword. His fingers touched the handle and then slowly his full hand grabbed the sword. Darian plunged it on the ground of the temple and now he didn't feel exhausted anymore and new energy reached every muscle of his body. Darian felt his heartbeat in his head.

The upholder looked at Darian with his brown eyes and after some time of silence, the upholder started to walk at him. He tried to crawl away, but soon his back touched the wall again. The upholder was coming closer and closer. With every further step Darian felt helpless. The upholder started to swing his staff, with only one single strike he would kill Darian. Darian raised his sword against the upholder and closed his eyes. *Lira, I'm so sorry, my love,* he thought and waited for the pain of death.

There was no pain. Instead there was darkness and Darian wagered, if he should open his eyes. At last he opened them and he looked at solid earth. *Is the world of the afterlife looking just like the normal world?*, then he looked around. His arm was still raised and in his hand was his sword. The upholder was standing next to him his staff was at his side. He was in a guarding position. Belric was watching everything from an entrance to the hall, on his face was a look of confusion. Darian turned his sword, so that the thin side of the blade was looking at the upholder. The upholder now moved into a fighting position, but he wasn't attacking Darian. Darian turned his sword so that the broad side of the blade was looking at the upholder. The upholder returned to his guarding position.

Darian slowly stood up and lowered his hand. The upholder was still standing and it seemed as if he wasn't moving any muscle, if such a creature as these actually have any muscles. Both Darian and Belric couldn't belief their own eyes. „What is this sorcery?", screamed Belric across the hall. Darian didn't say anything, „Ah I know. This is the secret of these temples. The power to control these giants.", Darian exchanged a look with Belric. On his face was a glimpse of his smirk. „With such a power, I could raise a kingdom of my own. I could kill all of my enemies and reign over every folk and thus I would not only be the most powerful man in this world, but also the wealthiest man alive. Gold and riches beyond measure. I only have to find out one thing: How to gain this power.", he smirked.

„You won't find it out, as you're a greedy person, who gets corrupted by a small glimpse of power or gold.", Darians face was like steel. Cold and hard, unlikely for Darian, but confronted with such a person he cannot hold his temper.

„If not, I shall take this power. Give it to me, Darian. Give it to me and maybe I'll share some of my riches with you."

„Not until my very last breath.", Belric started to approach Darian, his sword was still in his hands.

„So you want to keep this power for yourself? Darian, I'm disappointed, I thought you were a person, who shares with people in need, who doesn't take everything for himself. Then I'm glad, that I can end the life of such a vicious person.", Darian only felt anger for Belric, he wanted to corrupt Darian. Belric attacked Darian and their fight began anew.

They fought through the hall and the exhaustion returned. Blows from above, from downside, from the sides, twists and turns. Darian was cut on his left cheek and Belric on his left arm. Belric attacked with a blow straight to Darians shoulder. Darian leaned back turned his sword and pointed it at Belrics stomach. Belric stroked Darians sword from above and pushed him back, he followed with a kick to Darians stomach. Darian fell back and coughed. „What was that Darian? I thought you had a talent for fighting. But it seems, as if this talent fades away the longer a fight takes.", Darian was breathing heavily and he didn't know what to say, so he only stood up. „Seems like you haven't only lost your fighting talent, but also your voice!", he smirked.

The upholder started to move and he walked into the direction of Darian and Belric. Belric turned around and now both of them looked at the giant coming closer. He moved his staff to his right stone hand and started to swing it around. Once he came close to Belric, he started to swing the staff to his side and then the giant prepared for a strike at Belric. Belric was standing there like a solid rock, he didn't move.

The upholder started his attack at Belric. Belric was screaming loudly at the face of death coming at him. He didn't even raise his sword against the giant. Darian screamed a word too.

The giant was standing with his staff holding in front of Belrics face. The staff nearly touched his long brown beard. Belric was in a complete shock his eyes were only pointed at the staff in front of his eyes. Darian ran to Belric and flung Belrics sword across the room and punched him with his elbow to the head. Belric fell to the ground, not moving, but still breathing.

Darian turned his sword and the upholder returned to his guarding position. „Return, upholder of this ancient temple. I'm sorry, that such an ill person came inside this temple and that such foul words were spoken in this temple.", Darian looked to the ground and hinted a bow. The upholder returned to the place, where he once guarded the temple and waited for greedy persons. Darian however took a deep breath. *It's over,* were his thoughts.

Epilogue

He walked through a hallway. The hallway was covered in an orange color, as the glass of the windows had an orange color. On both sides were long silken banners. On them were seven stars on a green field. Guards with lances were standing on both sides. He walked through fifteen or more ranks of guards. In his right hand was a sword, the guards didn't took the sword away from him, as it is expected of him to have this sword with him. At the end of the hallway was a round room. Within this room were many pillars, between each pillar stood another guard with a lance. The pillars surrounded a big chair, furs were lying on the chair.

Next to the chair stood an elve, with a long bright green coat. His hair was brown and bound together behind his head. The color of his hair and his coat matched together and they reminded him of a forest during spring and it was supposed to be like this. The elve made a gesture to follow him. To outsiders the elve looked like a strict person, but actually he just followed his orders.

Together they walked through a door leading to another smaller hallway, but the hallway was still guarded by six guards in a more glamorous armor, than the guards in the bigger hallway and on the wall were now huge paintings of woods and landscapes. Every three paintings came a door on both sides. Both always passed the doors and walked on. They were walking on a colorful carpet. The watchful eyes of the guards stapled on both, observing every step and move.

At last they reached the end of the hallway, where another door was situated. The door didn't look special nor was it made out of a special material. The elve knocked at the door and gently opened it. Both stepped into the room and the elve closed the door again. The room had a big table made out of oak wood, around the table were many chairs. On the other side of the room was a bigger chair. It was made out of birch wood. Behind the chair was a window opened. You could only sparely see the city beyond it. Before the window stood another elve, with a long white robe. „Your highness, to you comes Darian from the realm of man. He has a gift for you.", said the elve, who first met Darian. The elve on the window turned his head away from the window and to the direction of Darian.

„Thank you Falis, you may leave us alone now.", said the elve at the window. The other elve bowed and left the room. Silence was in the room. Although there was no reason for it, Darians body was filled with tension. The elve left the window and walked around the table, coming closer to Darian. His face had the expression of interest and so was his movement, moderate and warily. He looked at the sword in Darians right hand and Darian stretched out his hands. Giving the sword to the elve.

„Your sword, your grace. You shall have it back.", he looked into the eyes of the elve.

„So it's done?", he asked and Darian replied with a nod. The elve grabbed the sword. He pulled out a little bit of the sword at first and inspected the sword. Then he pulled out the sword completely. „Looks just as I've given it to you. Tell me about it. What you found out about the legends."

„I can say you this: Some of them are true. There are temples for the elements and they are hidden in every corner of our world. But they don't keep any gold or riches. Instead they have traps for greedy persons, who are only after the gold mentioned in the legends. Then something happens within these temples, through which these greedy people mostly die. This is probably the reason why only few people know of these temples and the ones, who do know about them call them cursed. I believe the temples keep scripts and documents about an ancient folk."

„The Ancestors…", the elve interrupted Darian, „They're called the Ancestors or the First Elves. They probably built these temples. How did you find the temples?", the elve laid the sword on the table and returned to Darian.

„In a small elven town, to which I have traveled to very often, I have found records of a mad man, who presumably went into one of the temples. He drew some symbols, which arguably have shown the location of one of the temples. I followed these and they've led me to the valley of Eriandor. There I found the first temple and within every temple are markings to the other temples. I followed them and found every temple."

"Interesting, truly interesting.", said the elve.

"However I did encounter resistance. A host of men under the command of Belric Reever. They were out to find out the secret of these temples and to plunder them. Belric believed the legends about the gold and riches within the temples."

"Disastrous! These men have to be punished, for they wanted to plunder and damage the temples of my ancestors!"

"No, only one of them has to be punished and this one is already in your captivity, Belric Reever. The others only got manipulated by him and they either died or they fled. But I hope I can trust you not to kill Belric."

"We'll see.", he only responded, "Do the temples only keep the documents about the Ancestors or do they also keep something different?"

"Yes they do keep something else. They keep a secret power deep within them. A power, which your sword keeps from now on.", the elve looked at the sword on the table, "The temples are protected, not only by nature, but also through upholders. Creatures, giants made out of stone or ice. Once one of the traps is activated they become alive and kill the intruders. However they are bound to the power hidden inside the temples and this power can be absorbed by only one material."

„Steel of the Ancestors."

„Right and your sword has been made out of this steel and it's the heritage of your family. With your sword… you can now control these upholders of the elements.", Darian felt uneasy saying these last words. He looked deeply into the eyes of the elven king. He couldn't see anything change in his eyes and Darian felt a bit relieved.

„You know when I've first ordered you to search for these temples. I couldn't have imagined that you would come back with certain results nor with such a gift. I hesitated when I thought about giving you the sword of my family. But I trusted you and now you've come back with this gift.", he paused for a long moment. Darian didn't know if he should say anything, but he decided not to. At last he found words: „I don't know how I should thank you, for such a gift, Darian. Shall it be gold?"

Darian took a very deep breath. „No gold. I would only be satisfied if you give me your word. Your word to not use this power for foul reasons, not only for your own benefit. Belric wanted to use it for his own benefit and his plans with this power made me hesitate, that maybe I shouldn't tell you about this power. But now I'm asking you to give me your word.", the elve sighed.

„Darian you remember how nearly everything in this palace symbolizes the nature and it's beauty? The paintings, the colors. They're here to remind the elven king, what is the basis of his reign and what he should keep. Peace. Kings, who don't follow this guiding principle don't last very long. Only some kings got overthrown, but most kept the peace, as long as they've could. I give you my word: I shall only use this power to keep the peace and never use it for my own benefit. I promise it.", Darian didn't feel relieved.

„You are currently at war, your grace. The second one of your reign. You said an elven king rules to keep peace in the realm."

„We negotiated for many days with the dwarves, but they wouldn't listen and attacked us first. The first war was a war, which began during the reign of the king before me. He was overthrown, as he didn't even try to negotiate with the dwarves. I'm now currently doing everything I can to end the war, to keep the peace."

Now Darian felt relieved. To Darian it seemed, as if his words spoke the truth and he could see it in his eyes too. „Well then, your grace. I will leave now. I wish the best luck for you returning the peace and keeping it."

„Wait! Take this Darian.", he walked to the table and opened a small drawer. From it he pulled out a small bag. He gave it to Darian and Darian felt coins in it, but he didn't feel any satisfaction. „Farewell, Darian!". Darian opened the door and walked through it. Before closing it he turned around and said farewell to Honlarius, king of the elves.

He walked through the hallway and entered the throne room. Next to the throne stood Falis. Darian walked to him and whispered to him: „Tell the king this: I hate people, who break their promises.", then they said their goodbye. He felt the look of Falis, as he walked through the hallway and finally left the palace.

Darian was standing on top of a broad staircase, lowering into the life of the small folk of this big city. Before he started to walk down the stairs, he looked into the great city and it truly was great: Every here and there were huge trees rising into the clouds and between the trees were small houses. Unlike the great city of Krenn-so-ul where poor and wealthy are separated from each other, through the different layers of the city, the elves live a life with one another. Darian already saw wealthy elves spending food or gold to the poorer elves. The sellers would even sell their goods to the poorer elves with a smaller price, as these elves couldn't afford such high prizes. The dwarves would never do this, as the sellers are to greedy and they won't even sell so much within the first layer. Instead one can meet the most merchants within the second layer, but none in the third, as it's forbidden to sell anything there. But Darian didn't want to think about Krenn-so-ul and its problems, but rather he wanted to enjoy the beauty of Vasindrul.

The forest went on forever and the first time Darian watched at this view, he couldn't tell when the city ended and when the forest started and it is truly difficult to distinguish both of them. Darian started to walk down the stairs, at the end of the stairs waited four more guards of the elven king, but these were not the royal soldiers. The last one Darian would see in this city, as they only guard the royal palace. The rest of the city would be guarded by the city guard, but they can only be seen sparely on the street. Right after the staircase was a small bridge leading over a small artificial river, which flowed around the palace of the elven king. As he crossed the bridge he immediately got caught by the life of Vasindrul. Children playing on the street. Men exchanging friendly words. Families making appointments for their evening. Sellers pushing carriages loaded with leeks, cabbages, carrots, tomatoes, cucumbers and potatoes. The street divided for hundreds of times and each separation led to another separation. However Darian never took any separation, instead he walked on and on.

After even more separations and crossings, Darian walked into the great market of Vasindrul. Here the voices were so many and so loud, you wouldn't hear your own steps. Additionally birds sing a loud hymn in this region. The market is surrounded by six big trees and in the middle of the market is another tree, the biggest of the city. Its often called the tree of life. The trees are standing in the same order, as a constellation of stars. Six stars surrounding a star in the middle. The Seed or the Seed of the world, as it's called in a certain story.

The story suggests the world was created by six seeds. From the first seed developed the mountains, rocks and stones. The second released air into the world. From the third came the earth, dry and useless. So the fourth let loos of the water, to feed the earth. The fifth brought coldness to the world, so that the mountains had an ornament. But then there was no stability in the world any longer, so the sixth seed brought warmth back into the world in resemblance of fire. At last when the world was in balance again the last seed brought the life to the earth. Trees grew, animals accustomed to the world and it's balance. From the trees descended the first elves and they learned how important the nature is to this world. The trees are the offsprings of the seeds and the story turns even into a prophecy: Once the great tree in the middle dies or the star in the sky fades away, dead will come over the world. Many believe this is the way how the world got created and the first elves, the Ancestors, were born and this is why no one lives inside these trees. Darian however, thinks this is only partly true, as the story implements the six elements of this world, but Darian didn't know what to say about the prophecy. There was once a dark time, during which people waited for the tree to die or the star to fade away, but it did not happen. There is even a special festival, for the seven trees. It's called *Tsuri* and on this day nearly the whole market is empty (compared to the market on a normal day) and there are only few stands for food and drinks. The elves, would come to the market and sing and dance together, before the trees. This festival not only exists to honor the trees and their work, but also for the elves to remember, what makes it possible, to live in this world.

So Darian walked through the entire market and looked at all the different fruits and vegetables, which were showcased at the stands. Salmon from the Freed Island, trout from the Basilisk Islands, carp from the Moon Island. But there was not only fish, but also juicy apples from the realm of man near Goldkeep, acid lemons from Sandstone. Meat from *Quarils* and pigs of the dwarven realm. Besides food and drinks, you could also buy furs and wooden tools or furnitures. But also cloth was sold, together with silk carpets. There's only one market that could truly match the market of Vasindrul and that is the market of Landriel. Kids sometimes came running through the market, with joy in their faces and laughter filling the atmosphere. Darian was truly happy now, now that it was all over.

It wasn't long until Darian came to the great tree in the middle of the market. He looked from the bottom of the tree up to the branches. He even had to take some steps back to truly see to the branches. The sun was shining through the leaves and when he looked closely he could see the blue sky. Darians emotions reflected on the weather. He looked down again and then Darian saw her.

Looking into the streets of the market. Her hands fondling in her long black hair and clothed with a beige dress with green threads. She slowly turned to Darians direction and then their eyes met. Darian started to walk at her, his heart raced. As he reached her, she fell into his arms and they stood next to the great tree with a heartfelt hug.

„So you received my message?", Darian asked her.

„Yes. You can't imagine how happy I was, once I saw your name on it.", she said to him. They looked at each other, „Is it over?", she asked.

„Yes it is, Lira.", they smiled and kissed each other.

„What shall we do now?", Lira asked him.

„Well since it's your first time in Vasindrul, I think it would be appropriate for you to see the beauty of this city. So I shall tour you around extensively, for we now have all the time, that is given to us. After you've seen this city, I'd like to travel with you around this world. I've got some friends to visit. How does that sound to you?", she only smiled at him and then they kissed each other again.

The End

Authors note

A small notification from my side: the song at the beginning of the fifth chapter isn't a song of my own. Instead this song originally comes from „The Chieftains". The rights belong to „The Chieftains".

Also a very big thank you to all the people, that supported me throughout my writing process and encouraged me to finish this book! Without you this book would've never been published and for this I'm very grateful!

Zeitfracht Medien GmbH
Ferdinand-Jühlke-Straße 7
99095 Erfurt, Deutschland
produktsicherheit@kolibri360.de